I0831785

INTO A DREAM

Atlas Hill

Rhapsody Books

This is a work of fiction. All the characters, organisations, and events portrayed in this novel are either products of the author's imagination or are used fictitiously.

First published by Rhapsody Books in 2019

Copyright © Atlas Hill 2019

Atlas Hill asserts the moral right to be identified as the author of this work.

All rights reserved.

No part of this book may be reproduced in any form or by any electronic or mechanical means, including information storage and retrieval systems, without written permission from the author, except for the use of brief quotations in a book review.

Cover art by Caring Wong

ISBN 978-0-6482852-4-3

eBook ISBN 978-0-6482852-5-0

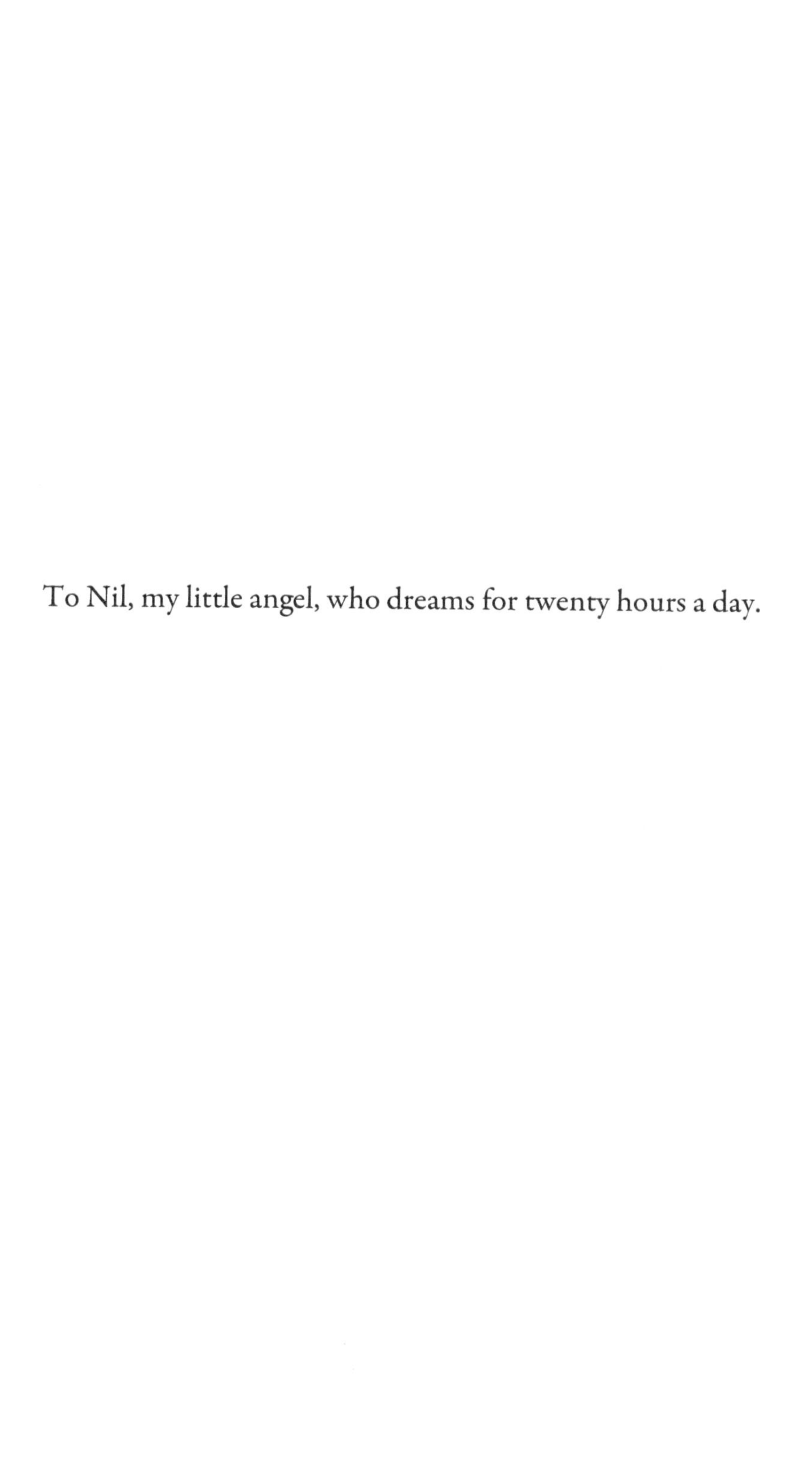

To Nil, my little angel, who dreams for twenty hours a day.

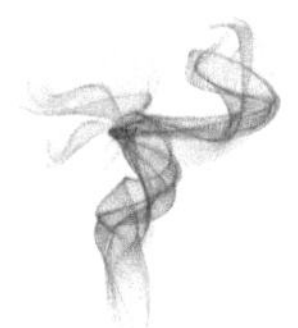

ONE

New York City, 2030

Some see nothing more than life and death. They are dead even in life, for they have no dreams. And yet when dreams die, does life essentially die, too?

This was the final event. Jess had performed tremendously well in the vault, the uneven bars, and the balance beam. But the floor exercise was the one event where the girl still made mistakes.

Cathy leaned forward and bit into her own lip, almost tasting blood. She couldn't help but share Jess's anxiety. The crowd was clapping to the beat of Dvořák's *New World Symphony*, an odd choice for artistic gymnastics, but a piece that perfectly matched Jess's expressive personality. It was impossible that this could go wrong, Cathy knew. But make no mistake, this was the climax. This was always the best part.

Jess was in the air, spinning in a connecting series of saltos, moving about as gracefully as the human body could manage—the routine harmoniously choreographed to the powerful symphony. Jess thumped back down to earth with a satisfactory landing, and immediately the girl was waving her arms and legs in sync with the music again, perfectly in tune with herself as she prepared for her next series of tumbling passes. Cathy gasped for breath as she watched Jess take in a deep breath of her own whilst performing a measured scale. A moment later, the young girl glided away with a handspring, leading to a cartwheel amid some boisterous applause—twisting and flipping in another series of crowd-pleasing passes.

Jess had saved the highest-degree-of-difficulty triple twist for last. She was already whirling in the air, as if flying. If she could manage another neat landing, the championship was hers. Silence filled the air suddenly, the incessant chanting at a brief interlude.

Cathy, too, held her breath as the girl's feet shifted in preparation for touchdown. She could almost see chalk dust explode as feet touched floor. And, to Cathy's delight, it was Jess's best landing yet. The audience roared to life immediately, raucous praise raining down on the podium.

Cathy sniffed as tears streamed from her eyes. She couldn't be prouder of Jess who was now bowing to the cheering crowd. The score was going to be announced in a minute, but the smiles on the judging panel together with the chorus of cheers from the other gymnasts said it all. Gold belonged to Jess, and that assured the girl of a place at the Olympics. Cathy could already imagine the—

Everything rapidly began to gray out.

No. What is this?

It was too early.

A blackout, then.

Cathy opened her eyes, the fluorescent lamp above blinding her briefly. The return was always disorienting—even after a year. She shook away her daze as best she could and then looked to her right to where Jess was still asleep, the girl's face adorned with a slight grin, her temples connected to simple electrodes. Cathy detached the electrodes on her own temples and smiled as she continued to eye Jess. At least the girl was still living her dream. Or *dreaming* her dream, for that matter. As Cathy's eyes naturally shifted down to the girl's prosthetic left leg, she was reminded that Jess's aspirations were impossible in reality. The escalator incident had robbed Jess of her greatest ambition. But in Dreamscape, she could dream her dream. It was the important first step in her path to recovery from clinical depression.

Cathy sighed softly, and then looked ahead through the large panoramic glass to the next room. Reuben didn't spare a glance over, attentive in monitoring Jess's dream, ensuring that the narrative moved along without deviations. The dream itself would run for another year or so—though, in reality, it wouldn't last for more several hours. Cathy herself, in sharing the girl's dream, had only been asleep for barely thirty minutes. And yet, she had been a non-participating, close observer for nearly half a year of Jess's struggles and eventual success on the national stage. Time was relative in dream-sharing, and it was the single best way to experience another's dreams.

Reuben was in his usual lab coat, his natural golden skin a perfect contrast to the spotless white garment, which was in turn without a single crease top to bottom. Her long-time friend turned boss was a naturally refined man, always well-presented, with an athletic figure to match and a supreme level of intellect. He had fittingly but ironically been called "dreamy" by a host of different people, especially younger women. And why wouldn't he be regarded as such when he was also exceedingly wealthy? Since founding the Dreamscape technology, he had earned his deserved share of monetary gain, much more than he could ever spend. But Reuben didn't regard financial income as a measure of success. He didn't seem to find money fulfilling, having donated the bulk of his gains to charities across the country. He wasn't even interested in recognition or acclaim from the general public, as he had rejected multiple offers to be nominated for the Nobel Prize.

Cathy couldn't pinpoint exactly what appealed to Reuben anymore. She had known him for a quarter of a century, but the man was still an enigma, a riddle that seemed impossible to solve. True, it had only been a year since their reunion here in New York—Cathy hardly knew anything about Reuben's experiences for the fifteen years prior, since his departure from Tennessee. Sometimes, Reuben was a complete stranger, someone who simply didn't allow anyone to share in his feelings. The only thing that Cathy was sure of was her admiration of the man.

To her right, Jess let out a sudden titter. The girl must still be enjoying her dream. Nothing could possibly go awry with Reuben in control, "operating" the dream in a station that resembled the cockpit of a commercial aircraft. He never seemed flustered by their clients' dreams, flicking switches without expression, piloting Dreamscape so effortlessly despite the intricate commands. The basic functions were much like on a media remote control including commands such as rewind, fast-forward, pause, play at two-times speed, and so on. All of these time-related functions did not affect the dream itself, but only in how it was displayed within the command center on the wall-to-ceiling widescreen. And as time was relative, these controls were rather necessary, especially the slow-play feature, which slowed the pace of the dream for the viewer. The experience of being the "dream pilot," though, was entirely different from being *in* the dream that Cathy had only just departed. From the cockpit, the dreams usually made much less sense.

Cathy sighed then, wiping away a tear. She had already

forgotten most of Jess's dream, but she still empathized deeply. Cathy didn't consider herself emotional, but for the year that she had worked here, she had had a hard time repressing her emotions. She doubted that many people could when sharing so deeply in another's dreams. Reuben certainly *did* empathize with their clients' desires, for he had been the one to accept or decline each client in the first place, who were handpicked from a lengthy list of applicants—this power now solely in the hands of Cathy herself since a month and a half prior. Still, Reuben was perhaps the only person in the world, Cathy suspected, who seemed to share no part in anyone's actual dreams.

"You can go," Reuben said, bobbing his head slightly away from the controls and meeting Cathy in the eyes. "I'll finish up."

He was speaking through the microphone, of course, and the soft volume that sounded from the speakers wasn't loud enough to wake Jess from her state of deep sleep.

Cathy returned a tired but grateful nod. It had been a long day. Jess was the third client of the day and Cathy had shared all three dreams. It was not even 6:00 pm yet, but she couldn't imagine any other job that was more exhausting—to the mind, anyway.

She stepped out of the Dreamer's Lair and moved along the corridor toward the foyer. Toby, the young, bubbly receptionist, had gone home. The lights had been dimmed to indicate that the clinic was closed for the day. Only the video surveillance monitor was still on, which showed herself on screen one, Jess's family in the waiting room on screen two, Jess herself inside the Dreamer's Lair on screen three, and finally, Reuben and the command center on screen four. Reuben would ask Jess's family to leave in about two hours' time. After all, they were merely watching Jess's physical presence from the waiting room rather than sharing in the girl's dream. They would return early the next day to leave with Jess. They would then all finally be able to move on.

As she exited the clinic, Cathy eyed the poster on the left wall, a quote in large text backdropped by a night sky tinged with violet and illuminated by thousands of stars.

Who looks outside, dreams; who looks inside, awakes.

A quote by Carl Jung. A quote Cathy related deeply with.

Cathy rode the elevator, descending thirty-three floors. She stepped out from the building to the evening street adorned by decorous lampposts. She paused after a few steps at the cool breeze sweeping past her, brushing up gently falling snowflakes into her face. Like every winter in New York City, there were evenings like this: peaceful and romantic, despite the chill. Cathy nodded up, past the skyscrapers, and toward the sky which was polluted by artificial light. Stars were rarely visible in the city, unlike the poster in the foyer. On this evening, she would have to be content with only the glowing moon, its waning crescent looming over everything.

Dreams, she thought with a sigh then, her breath immediately fogging in the cold air. *Every dream has its worth ... you've said. And it is your dream that makes all others possible.*

She smiled and then headed toward the train station. She would have to stop by the drugstore to pick up some cough medicine for Reuben. However brilliant he might be, Reuben was still only human, still susceptible to common illnesses. It didn't help that he was a natural taskmaster. Whether he would accept the medicine or not was a question in itself, but Cathy would rather have it ready.

TWO

Painting One's Life

Better late than never, they say. Better yet is that it's never too late. Except when it is. Proverbs don't always apply. When things are over, they're over. Second chances are a privilege, not a right. Grasp onto every opportunity you get.

The first client of the day was Sofia Hoffman, a widow in her sixties. Many observers, if they knew about this, would have been confounded by two things. Firstly, what an elderly lady was doing here—what dreams could she possibly have at her age?—and secondly, why she had been granted the privilege at all.

It was true that the clinic had rarely seen clients over the age of forty since operations had begun nearly a year ago. Reuben had relinquished control of the client selection process to Cathy nearly a month prior, and Sofia was one of the last clients he had handpicked. Cathy was proud and honored to be given the reins, though at the same time saw the acceptance and prioritization of clients as a tough task. There were simply too many people who needed help, deserved it, and could hardly wait any longer. Reuben, though, had a more critical task to attend to, which was to further improve the technology of Dreamscape.

In any case, Cathy wasn't at all surprised that Reuben had chosen Sofia as a client and essentially granting her wish. The application form explained that Sofia had specialized in the romanticism style of traditional painting. She apparently possessed the skills to become a professional artist, but circumstances had been unkind to her.

"Good morning, Mrs. Hoffman," Cathy greeted, inviting the elderly lady, who was accompanied by a younger woman, into the Dreamer's Lair. "Congratulations on being selected. Please take a seat and allow me to explain the process for today."

Cathy gestured the elderly lady inside and toward the snuggly, round accent chair, which was a single-person sofa in a cozy room rather than a simple swivel chair one would expect to see in a medical clinic. Today's design of the Dreamer's Lair—from the furniture to the color, to the ambience, to the mildly musky aroma, and to the overall arrangement—was strikingly similar to a living room page out of a *Pottery Barn* catalog. It was homely, and this was critical in allowing their clients to feel as comfortable as possible prior to each dream. In this sense, Reuben had said they should always strive to be "invisible." Given that dreams were fed by the mind, especially of recent events, the more one was impressed upon at the clinic, the greater the risk of dream digression. And to that end, the entire arrangement of the room was customizable. Alternate furniture was stored in the next room, as were a variety of scented oils. The lighting could be adjusted, and even the walls changed colors at the press of a button. Even so, Reuben had also said that it was impossible for anyone to feel *completely* comfortable.

Judging from the open-mouthed expressions as their eyes wandered about the enclosure, Cathy was sure that both Sofia and the younger lady accompanying her were impressed by the setting, but not in the way that it would elicit unnecessary emotions that might distract their minds.

"Ah, thank you," the younger lady said, apparently at a brief loss for words, now finally reaching out for a handshake. "I'm Christine. The daughter."

Cathy had already learned from the application form that Christine Hoffman was a world-renowned pianist. She was perhaps a few years younger than Cathy herself, but she was already widely acclaimed for her interpretation and performance of Liszt's works. Although Reuben didn't favor the famous or even the talented, a large proportion of their clients *were* rich and famous. It was the wealth, the fame, and ultimately, the high social standing that bumped up some of these applications to the selection pool that they accessed. After all, the selection pool itself was managed by a third-party organization.

"Cathy Reed," Cathy offered, accepting the pianist's handshake and remembering that Christine had elected to be an observer only, and strictly so. Christine would share her mother's dream but would otherwise be invisible to her mother throughout, much in the same way that Cathy would sometimes share dreams in spectator-mode, too, for the purposes of technology maintenance.

Cathy nodded at Sofia, who had now settled into her upholstered seat. "Please make yourself comfortable."

Sofia blinked a couple of times and then met Cathy's eyes. "Will you really help me achieve my dream?" she asked with tremendous anticipation, her eyes glistening with tears. "Is it really possible?"

"Not that we're doubting you," her daughter inserted nervously. "We're just not very well-versed in these...uh, psychiatry practices."

"Worry not," Cathy assured with a smile, turning back to the elderly lady again. "It's all rather simple, actually. After hypnosis, you will enter Dreamscape. And from there, your aspirations will then feed into your mind, which when driven by our algorithms, will translate into your desired dream. The dream will be monitored from our side, but only to ensure that things run without interruptions."

Sofia squeezed hard onto her daughter's hand, clearly anxious about potentially achieving her ambitions after waiting for more than thirty years. Christine returned a gentle smile and patted her mother's hand.

"Christine, can I get you to sit here?" Cathy asked, motioning at the adjacent chair of the same design and comfort. "You can share your mother's dream by attaching the electrodes to your temples."

Christine nodded hesitantly and then fell into the round chair. She seemed to appreciate that family members weren't always allowed entry into the Dreamer's Lair, and that she had been given the privilege. She connected the electrodes as instructed and her mother followed her lead.

"Relax," Cathy said. "I'll be in the next room." She nodded at the artificial window they were all facing, which in actuality, was a large glass pane shared with the command center similar in function to the one-way mirrors in interrogation rooms. More advanced than those found in police departments, however, the glass here was indeed a high-tech screen which could display almost anything but could also function as a simple transparent window.

"Actually, we're about as relaxed as we can be," Christine said, reaching to her right to hold her mother's hand again.

"I'm more than fine," Sofia said, clearly eager to begin.

Cathy nodded at them once more, stepped out of the room, and traversed to the command center. The face-scan at the entrance took a second to validate her features, and upon recognition, the door slid open in a fashion not dissimilar to fictional spaceships in sci-fi films she had watched as a child. While it was still cool to experience a futuristic door almost every day, Cathy understood the security system must never be compromised, and that it was not at all for show.

Behind the door was, of course, the state-of-the-art circular command center, which might be seen as garish by some. Consistent with the spaceship-like entry, the command center was ornamented by a host of brightly lighted controls, switches, and a domed ceiling of connecting, curved widescreens which displayed the various status reports of the current dream. It really was like the cockpit of a fictional spaceship, albeit without any steering device—not literal steering, anyway. It wasn't all that large, with a capacity of only three people, though Cathy didn't think there had ever been more than two inside at any time. All of it, the technology and the design, was Reuben's creation.

Cathy caught the very man—billionaire, philanthropist, and pioneer of neo-psychotherapy—for barely a second before he spun away from her, his long lab coat flapping away behind him, as he coughed a few times. His cold just didn't seem to go away.

Cathy stepped in, not bothering to ask if he was well, imagining that Reuben would wave away her concern. She had offered him the cough medicine earlier in the morning, only to be reprimanded for being nosy. After a moment, Reuben spun back to her.

"You're up," he simply said, rising from his seat, in essence vacating it for her as he himself dropped onto the co-pilot seat opposite.

This was only the third time that Cathy had been entrusted to pilot a dream, but she felt little pressure. Reuben's trust in her ability gave her more confidence than she ever needed, and her excessive experience as a co-pilot—essentially sharing Reuben's perspective—had provided her with all the skills necessary to keep dreams afloat. She knew exactly how to deal with emergencies, which were rare to start with. After all, Dreamscape was fueled by the user's inner desires. The technology behind it, which Cathy couldn't say she knew too much about, was there only to help make the connection. In other words, the dream was mostly on autopilot, and Cathy imagined it was much less complicated than flying an aircraft. The autopilot mode itself was of course carefully programmed by Reuben himself, which meant that even as the pilot, her hand was being closely held along the way.

"I'm glad for her, for Mrs. Hoffman," Cathy said, pushing onto the hypnosis command, seeing mother and daughter close their eyes now through the large glass.

"As you are for all clients," Reuben responded dryly, followed with another cough.

Cathy said nothing for a moment, waiting for Reuben to say more, certain that he would.

"I am, too," Reuben then finally added. "Let's begin."

In the Dreamer's Lair, Sofia and her daughter had fallen asleep, as confirmed by the small "unconscious" signal displayed on the ceiling screen, which was now filled with beautiful illuminations of colorful nebulae floating among an infinite expanse together with millions of stars. According to Reuben, this galactic scenery and anything that resembled it was an image of the human mind which served as the entrance to one's dreams—the gateway to the unconscious.

Beyond the nebula was the beginning of Sofia's dream. It all began in a series of non-sensical, fast-moving, abstract images, which floated about rather randomly. About ten seconds in, Cathy turned the time knob to slow the dream on display to match real time. This, of course, wouldn't affect the actual dream itself, which would continue to run at its own speed.

In first-person mode, as was displayed on-screen, it could be difficult to determine the role that the client played—such as how old they were. From the mostly wooden Eames-esque furniture in the scene, Cathy guessed it was a house in the sixties that Sofia was floating in and gradually landing upon. Her small hands were that of a child. And not surprisingly, the next significant item that appeared in the murkiness was a painting set including a traditional palette, brushes, canvas, and an easel. As Sofia stroked gently onto the canvas, a soft tune—one of Beethoven's sonatas—played in the background from a large burgundy box which would today be regarded as a valuable turntable.

"I once wanted to be an artist," Reuben said, his sudden remark almost making Cathy start. Reuben rarely shared any stories, and rarer that he shared them in the middle of a dream.

"Not the traditional kind," Reuben continued. "More of a digital artist."

Cathy cleared her throat. "What made you change your mind?"

"My mother."

Silence filled the air for more than a moment as Cathy searched for a response. She was glad that they were sitting away from one another, an arrangement that saved her shocked expression from being seen. This was the first time in a long time that Reuben had spoken about something on a personal level. And that wasn't even the strangest part. She didn't know when exactly, but Cathy was sure that Reuben's mother had died long ago along with his father. He would have only been a toddler at the time.

"She was a digital artist," Reuben clarified. "I was seven when I learned about it. She was good, but it never went anywhere."

"She didn't receive recognition for her work?" Cathy asked.

"None."

"I'm sorry," Cathy said. "I don't know what to say, but perhaps we should—"

"I didn't mean to bore you," Reuben interrupted. "I'll keep quiet now."

Cathy immediately regretted her choice of words. She opened her mouth again, hoping to urge Reuben to share more. But, after a pause, a sigh was all she managed.

After roughly three quarters of an hour in real time, Sofia had achieved her dream to be a professional painter and had now lived about five years into the success. In between, Cathy and Reuben also learned from the dream that in reality the woman had lost her husband in a traffic accident almost thirty years ago, shortly after their daughter was conceived. Prior to the tragic incident, Sofia Hoffman worked off her husband's money as a hugely promising artist, gifted especially in oil painting, and was even accepted into the Rhode Island School of Design as a student. Of course, she had later been forced to give up her dream altogether and settle for a much less rewarding career in labor jobs when faced with financial shortage and the need to raise her daughter single-handedly. It was perhaps fate that it was her daughter, Christine, who was now an established pianist herself, happily married, bringing her loving mother to live the dream she deserved.

It was lovely to see. Anyone sharing this moment would be brought to tears of joy.

Cathy, stop her, a voice seemed to murmur.

"Cathy!"

Reuben brushed Cathy aside from behind and flicked several switches in quick succession, glaring eyes never leaving the dream on display. Having immersed herself too deeply into the dream, Cathy finally realized now that Christine had been attempting to step into an active role, into her mother's vision within the dream. Cathy rose to her feet and stepped back a little more to give Reuben space. As she swallowed a lump in her throat together with the guilt of potentially causing chaos within an otherwise perfect dream, she found some relief in noting that everything was soon under control again, but with Christine ejected from the dream altogether. Glancing through the window, she saw that the pianist remained in slumber.

"Her sleeping state is maintained," Reuben said, eyes still on the screen, breathing a soft sigh of relief himself. "I believe that she merely wanted to share in her mother's joy. It is dangerous, however."

"I'm sorry," Cathy said, ashamed, unable to find any excuses for her lapse of concentration.

"Human error is expected," Reuben said, finally meeting

Cathy's heated eyes. "Not to worry, though, not in this instance. But Cathy, please step out for a moment. Have a rest. Do not return until the clients depart."

It was an hour later when Reuben fetched Cathy from the breakroom, reassuring her that the dream had been a success, and that both Sofia and her daughter were delighted with the experience. As they exited the room, Cathy trailed Reuben, at that instance suddenly awed again by his physical stature despite only being a few inches taller than her. Born to a white mother and a black father, his skin was a natural golden, shimmering as if a saint.

Truth be told, appearance had little to do with it. It was his very presence, almost as if an aura of greatness permeated his surroundings, that aura leaving a trail of grace behind him everywhere he went. It was ironic that he was often described by many women as "dreamy" when he actually had the ability to make every one of their dreams come true, no matter what they might be. In a world constantly marred by sins and tragedies, Reuben was a beacon of hope, a man who could always be relied upon to ascend the rest of them into a new world.

Reuben paused abruptly as he reached the foyer, Cathy almost bumping into him from behind. The lights were still on. A middle-aged man, well-groomed with a neat stubble, stood at the reception with a squint pointed at Reuben. He sported a simple sweater and carried a trench coat on his left arm.

"Apologies, Mr. Granger," Toby, the receptionist, said, "but this gentleman, Mr. Sullivan, refused to leave until he saw you. He said that he knew you personally, so ..."

"Granger," the man addressed Reuben with a tilt of his head, "it's been a while."

Cathy glanced at the stranger and then back toward Reuben, who seemed to be placing him.

"I do not believe I can help you," Reuben then finally said, little emotion attached.

"And I did not expect your cooperation," Sullivan inserted, lifting his chin before a smirk spread across his face. "No matter. I'll close this place down soon enough."

An immediate pang of annoyance stung within Cathy. Just who was this Sullivan? And how dare he speak to Reuben like that? A lawyer? A competitor? Or, was this somehow a dream? If in the case that—

"You're not welcome here," Toby said, finally breaking the stalemate.

Cathy glanced over at her young colleague, relieved and also impressed that he was able to be stern when the situation called for it. The only regret was that she hadn't been the one to deliver that simple yet effective statement.

"I imagined that you might be hostile," Toby continued, reaching for the phone on his desk. "Mr. Granger, should I call security?"

"Not necessary," Reuben said, eyes still locked onto Sullivan. "He's an old friend ... who will be leaving in a moment."

"I'm honored," Sullivan said with a shake of his head. "And, Granger, we still *can* be friends, that is, as long as you cooperate with me. I just need you to—"

"You're mistaken," Reuben said, cutting Sullivan off. "I consider you a friend of the past, Jeremy. Nothing more. But given our brief history, and also your highly esteemed role as a research fellow, I wish not to humiliate you by having you escorted away."

"Stubborn as always, I see," Sullivan responded with a sneer. "You leave me with no choice, then." He paused and then surveyed the room for a moment, as if probing for any possible flaws—perhaps cracked walls or a collapsing ceiling? "You're here trying to run a psychiatry clinic," he then said. "But with no license. One call to the New York State Medical Board, and you're done. I'll have you shut down within weeks."

Cathy jerked slightly at the threat. New York State Medical Board? What was this about having no license? This man was out of his mind, surely. It was an empty threat, and yet the thought itself was outrageous. This was already the second mention of a shutdown, and while Reuben didn't seem perturbed at the slightest, the acute anger inside Cathy was roaring to new heights.

"Call anyone you want," Reuben said, calm as always, gesturing now to the exit. "But it's getting late. My staff need rest."

Sullivan glanced over at Cathy then. "So, this is her, eh?" Sullivan said. "Cathy Reed. I truly hope she's not Vanessa's replacement."

It was only subtle, but Reuben tightened on the mention of Vanessa, not a name Cathy was familiar with. More importantly, Cathy thought that she saw a tinge of ire in Reuben, an emotion she didn't think he was capable of—at least not since their reunion. And that triggered a distinct fear in Cathy. Only in her wildest fantasies had she ever imagined the potential of Reuben's wrath.

"Toby, call security," Reuben asked with a change of mind, this instruction drawing a cringe from Sullivan.

"I'm on it!" the young man obliged with pleasure, prompt in dialing.

"I won't allow anyone to disrespect Cathy," Reuben said in clarification of his new stance.

The fear Cathy had been feeling only seconds ago vaporized immediately, all of that suddenly replaced with an all-encapsulating warmth that caressed every part of her body and soul. She had always believed that Reuben cared for her, and though it was only a simple gesture, his defense of her completely melted her heart. Cathy was almost sure that she was blushing, her cheeks burning. Probably a rosy pink had sprouted to view beneath the thin layer of foundation.

"I've said what I had to," Sullivan said with a hiss, finally spinning for the exit. "Consider this a forewarning, Granger," he said as he receded. "I'll do everything in my power to stop this madness."

The security guards, two of them, arrived at the entrance soon enough. The double glass doors slid open on a simple swipe of the card they brought with them, and they then trampled in toward Sullivan, who conceded defeat and departed with reluctance.

THREE
Limitations

Like most things, technology is wonderfully dangerous and dangerously wonderful at the same time. Regardless, it's not technology we need to be wary of, but the people who access the technology. The greatest inventors in history likely predicted how their inventions could be used or misused, but how many of them would expect their inventions might one day destroy mankind as we know it? Being hopeful is admirable but let us remember that it takes one bad apple to spoil the bunch.

It had been a week since his visit, and Sullivan never came back. Business had been running as usual with the usual concoction of stress, heartbreak, touching moments, and pride. Reuben had said no word about his old acquaintance. He was still coughing, and it was getting worse. But Cathy didn't wish to be reprimanded once again for prying. She did find consolation, though, in the fact that Reuben had gone home early today, allegedly to "take care" of his aggravating condition. Whether or not that was going to happen, it was good for Reuben to be someplace else other than at work.

In any case, Cathy was still glad about Sullivan, that he hadn't shown again. It was as if he had never set foot in their building. For the sake of the clinic and its clients, Cathy hoped that he would never appear again.

"Michael's just about to wake up," Cathy said, passing the client's file to Toby. "Please lock up when he's done. Can you also make sure the backup power is on?"

She watched the monitor in front of Toby, which showed live footage divided into four parts: the foyer, the waiting room, the Dreamer's Lair, and the command center.

"You know, Ms. Reed," Toby said, eyes also on the monitor, fingers running across the keyboard, "I've never seen the backup power actually used. Will there *ever* be a need for it? Just saying."

"Probably not," Cathy agreed. "But better to be safe than sorry."

"This is the Zenith Tower, but!" Toby insisted. "It's the most technologically advanced building in New York, and possibly the world. *And*, they even have their own backup power system which would kick-in if it detects even the slightest possibility that the main power fails. This system of ours is a backup of a backup. I'm telling you. It would never happen!"

"Mr. Granger's instructions," Cathy said with an innocent smile and a shrug. She tapped her finger on the palm-sized security screen adjacent to Toby's monitor, which began to scan her hand. A second later, the options popped out as a beautiful blue hologram, floating in front of them. The backup power was already on, of course, as indicated by the green "'activated" signal. Cathy smiled and then pinched away the menu, sending the program to sleep.

"I'm off, Toby," Cathy said, flapping on her trench coat.

"Actually, Miss Reed, someone left you a voice mail."

Cathy raised a brow. It was rare to leave voice mails, especially at the clinic whose number wasn't publicized. Anyone who knew Cathy personally could simply call her on her cell. Toby looked reluctant to say much more, his face marred by a slight pout as he tapped the "play" button on his screen. Cathy swallowed, praying that it wasn't Sullivan.

Hey Cath, it's me, Beth, said the recorded voice, its familiarity bringing immediate relief. *Didn't mean to catch you here, but I lost your latest number. I'm in town for several days. And hey, just to get to you, I had to jump through all the hoops to get this number. Now consider—*

Cathy looked at Toby for an explanation of the abrupt ending. She couldn't be sure, but the tapping at the end which cut out the message sounded like someone picking up the phone.

"Yeah, sorry," Toby said with a guilty shrug. "I intercepted the call."

"Why?"

"Well ..." he said, pinching out Beth's caller ID hologram from the screen, which then expanded out into a 1/20 scale model hovering above the monitor. "Look at her," he said, referring to the model of Beth in a swimsuit carrying a surfboard in glorious augmented reality.

Toby was referring to Beth's beauty and alluring curves, of course. And it was true, Cathy agreed, that Beth was incredibly photogenic and yet even more striking in person. Her best friend had been living in California for a few years now. She had seen swimsuit holograms of her that were even more enticing.

"She's my age," Cathy said, biting on her lip to restrain a grin.

"I don't actually know how old you are, Ms. Reed," Toby said. "But I'd date you for sure."

"I'm flattered," Cathy said, shaking her head. "Let's just say

Beth and I are a tad mature for you. She's a neurosurgeon."

Beth suggested meeting at a bar. It was Friday evening, after all. Despite all the stress of modern-day life in New York City, it was *the* time to let loose. The dim lighting of the establishment and the soft instrumental music playing in the background positioned itself as a posh bar, likely with steep prices to match. But the somewhat woolgathering atmosphere and ambience upon stepping inside the enclosure washed over Cathy with the familiarity of Dreamscape. Even after a year, there were still times when she had trouble distinguishing reality from Dreamscape, and from her actual dreams. There was a thin line between daydreaming and lucid dreaming, and sometimes—as she was now—it felt like she was floating somewhere in between. Cathy appreciated establishments that evoked particular moods, and this bar was certainly one of them.

Beth was sitting at the bar. She had always preferred it, if not for the convenience, then certainly for the joy of being shone upon by the glittering selection of alcohol. And as always, Beth was gorgeous, her straight bangs and long curls of blonde cradling her face, which wore a slight whimsical smirk. The other constant about Beth was that she was never without a date—on this evening, she was with a well-groomed man with short dark hair and medium stubble in a dark blue dress suit.

"It's been a while, Bethany," Cathy called out as she approached them, beaming at her, already opening her arms for a hug.

"Oh, Cath," Beth said with delighted surprise, stepping to her feet for a warm embrace. "It's so great to see you." She turned to her companion and introduced him as Jackson, adding that, "he's one of *them*."

Jackson chortled, shaking his head. "Yes, I am indeed. But Cath, I promise I'll help safeguard your details for as long as I'm around."

"A pleasure," Cathy said, receiving his hand for a handshake. The disgust she felt for him was immediate. "But please call me Cathy," she said. "Cath is reserved for only a few people."

The relentless dread she and most other good people of the world were subject to was the result of those working in Jackson's profession. This man was a professional tracker, someone that Beth should look at with contempt as much as she did. People like Jackson was the very reason why Cathy had to change numbers all the time. They were notorious for abusing all kinds of privacy and most commonly for recording sound from one's device and, in some cases, even video. One had to ensure they were well-protected at sensitive times, including when giving out new numbers to friends and family. Cathy was especially careful given that she worked at the clinic. Beth, meanwhile, was a medical professional like her, who couldn't afford compromising client details and therefore should be staying away from the likes of Jackson altogether.

"Give this one a martini, will you?" Beth asked the young bartender as Cathy settled on the stool next to her friend.

The bartender winked in response and then slid away to prepare her drink. Beth herself had a Long Island Iced Tea, her usual choice when she was in New York. Jackson had the Manhattan, likely only to play alongside Beth's choice.

"So, Cathy," Jackson said with a contemptible grin, "Beth tells me you work in some kind of clinic."

"Are you *really* asking?" Cathy said, trying to sound satirical rather than plain rude. "You didn't look me up? You don't already know *everything* about me?"

The tracker chuckled, shaking his head. "You're a blunt one," he remarked, drawing Cathy's ire even more. "Look, I take my profession seriously, but I also know the meaning of respect. I won't deny that I looked you up when Beth said that we were seeing you, but barely ten percent of your data was available, and I didn't even pry through all of that."

"Wow," Cathy said outright sarcasm. "You have my gratitude."

"Be nice, Cath," Beth finally said, sitting forward between them. "Jackson's not like the rest of them. *I* trust him and I ask you to at least try."

Cathy met Beth's eyes and saw earnestness in them. She knew her friend didn't usually defend men with such solemnity, but Cathy didn't know for sure. After all, she usually found Beth's romantic partners inconspicuous rather than irritable. After a moment, Cathy shifted her gaze back to Jackson, who regarded her in turn.

"Sorry," Cathy said, trying her best to sound sincere, "about my premature judgement."

"You are forgiven," the tracker responded with a grin slightly less contemptible, perhaps due in part to Beth's glowing smile that always radiated everything in the vicinity. "Now, to make it fair," Jackson continued, "let me *reveal* a few details about myself."

He stressed the word "reveal" for good reason. In order to survive the competition, trackers were extremely careful in hiding their true identity, mostly against other trackers. Cathy had never personally met anyone in the profession, at least not knowingly, but she knew that it was a big deal for Jackson if he really were to share any personal details.

"Jackson's not my real name," he began, clipping the stem of his drink, looking into the transparent liquid as he swirled it about. "The real me died many years ago. I'll say this, Cathy Reed," he said, speaking in a sudden whisper, "*I despise trackers so much more than you do.*"

He scowled wordlessly for a moment, as if to allow the information to sink in. He wouldn't know that Cathy wasn't yet convinced, that she didn't trust easily, especially trackers whose supreme lying skills were part of their job description.

Jackson then sighed softly, his scowl transforming into a jaded expression as he lifted his head toward the liquor selection before the bar. "It's true," he continued. "I lost *everything* to them. But to survive, I chose to become one of them. To say I'm ashamed is an understatement."

Beth rested her hand on his forearm to console him, a gesture that he seemed to appreciate and perhaps even deserve if his story were true.

"This is no movie," Cathy found herself saying, hearing the distinct cynicism in her own tone. "Don't tell me you're trying to take some kind of revenge or that your goal is to uproot all the trackers in the world."

Jackson and Beth turned to her, the latter wearing a disapproving frown. Cathy regretted her words then but failed to apologize.

"I get this a lot," Jackson said with a smug grin. "Hostility, that is. But Cathy Reed, you do seem a tad sensitive about my profession. And I can't even say why."

"It's been barely a half hour since he knew we were meeting you, Cath," Beth said. "Jackson really doesn't know much about you."

"Well, not yet," Cathy responded, still unable to extend much courtesy toward the tracker.

"Look, Cath," Beth continued, placing her hand on Cathy's wrist, "I called you to catch up. To laugh. To relax. Come on. Let loose a little, will you?"

Cathy bit her lip, unable to respond with words just yet. Her growing feeling of guilt was building a lump in her throat. Beth had been impressively polite to her despite her unwarranted prejudice against Jackson. Beth was more rational than she had ever been, and the reason for her sensibility seemed to be Jackson, who had also been well-mannered.

"Cathy," Jackson said invitingly, pointing to the corner behind the bar where a man was playing darts. "Want a game?"

Cathy watched the dart player behind his headset—more like aviator sunglasses these days—holding onto the dart-shaped controller, following the typical motion and then hitting slightly to the left of bullseye as displayed on the circular monitor, scoring a twenty-five.

"Sorry, I'm not a fan of virtual reality," Cathy said, finally able to remove the scorn in her tone. "It gives me headaches."

"This coming from someone who works with dreams?" Beth asked with a raised brow, tone still playful.

"I agree they're quite different, actually," Jackson said before Cathy could respond. "Virtual reality has come a long way since its inception more than half a century ago. The *reality* part of the equation is nothing short of amazing—the very reason that more and more people prefer spending time in the virtual world than the real world. Hell, virtual currency is sometimes worth more than real money."

"I hear that they have a virtual New York City now," Cathy added, pondering the idea with a grin. "There could be virtual replicas of me and you."

"There are," Jackson affirmed. "Well, at least I'd assume so, Cathy—that you're there, too. I know for certain that Beth and I are there."

He winked at Beth then, who returned a smile with a shake of her head. "Anyway, Cathy," Jackson said, turning his attention to her again, "I'd like to know your thoughts. I can't say that I know much about this dream clinic you work at, but I think I can assume a thing or two about how it works."

"And what is it that you assume?"

Jackson shrugged. "Well, for one thing, it's a form of digital technology."

Cathy's lips curled up slightly, unsure whether or not she wanted to educate the tracker.

"But unlike virtual reality," Jackson continued, speaking before Cathy could comment, "the technology used at the dream clinic relies *not* on a set of programmed codes with which the world is created. In this way, the dream world is infinitely larger than anything possible in virtual reality as there is no limit of *storage* capacity. I'd assume that the basis of the dream world is the human mind, which is still far superior to computers in many ways. Even so, there would be certain limits governing all of this."

Cathy swallowed the lump that had built in her throat. "And what might these limits be?"

"One's physical energy, I suppose," Jackson said. "People need to eat, so they can't dream forever." He chuckled there. "Actually, that's really the same as VR, except that VR users have to sleep, too."

Cathy squinted at the tracker then. "I sense that you wanted to say more?"

Jackson returned the squint. "The other limit to the dream world is perilous," he said teasingly, showing teeth. "While the dream world, in theory, is close to limitless in what one could do and experience, the danger is the lack of a reset code. Modern virtual worlds are enormous, but they're still bound to a defined territory, which can be considered somewhat of a safety zone. The dream world, on the other hand, is like floating in space, in an infinitely wide expanse that knows no bounds." He paused and clipped onto the stem of his cocktail again. "In other words," he continued in a whisper, "one could easily get trapped within forever. One could die."

FOUR

Maryville, 2007

Reminiscence can be beautiful. The nostalgia magically brings us back to a "better, simpler" time. Such great visions, however, might well be fabrications, artificially created from how we wish to remember.

Reuben had stopped at the top of the slope, looking ahead to the view across the range, a view that would certainly have been spectacular behind the tangerine sky of dawn. Cathy's legs, though, were battling exhaustion and almost refusing to pedal on. They had been cycling for hours on largely steep and rough terrain. While her peers would consider her relatively fit, this was an adventure for seasoned cyclists—not Cathy Reed, a high school freshman who was above average in sport. She could hardly repress the envy she had for the other tourists arriving at the same destination, but in the comfort of their air-conditioned cars. The annoyance she felt for them was also more acute than she had expected. She had dreamed to share the landscape of Newfound Gap with only Reuben, but now after a grueling ride, she was rewarded with the unwanted companionship of many faceless bodies.

Among the crowd who was enjoying the view and snapping shots, Reuben spun back from the ascension and shot her an encouraging smile. He seemed fresh still, somehow. Evidently, intelligence wasn't his only attribute—he was athletic, too, and supremely so.

Cathy sighed and then stepped off the bicycle. It was easier to walk it up to the viewing platform. In the back of her mind, she was already dreading the long journey back to Gatlinburg. She had never even considered asking her parents to drive out here, which would most certainly ruin her alone time with Reuben. But now in her exhaustion, she remembered that she had no way of communicating with them anyway, not after dropping—and "bricking"—her cell in the creek earlier in the afternoon. The family was back at the cabin about thirteen miles away. Cathy almost felt treasured when Reuben dived into the stream to retrieve her cell, only to realize afterward that he merely didn't wish for the plastic to pollute the current. Still, Cathy was sure to keep the dysfunctional device as a memento of this trip.

Reuben offered a hand upon her final steps of catching up to him. The panorama was indeed spectacular atop the viewing platform. The Smokies was the most visited national park in the country, after all. Monumental hilly shapes of green were ahead for as far as one could see, the fog hanging over the landscape presenting itself in a way as if it were breathing life unto the earth. All of this was adorned by the mostly clear sky. Despite the crowds invading their personal space now, Cathy was thankful that she had shared the journey through the fragrant woodlands in which Reuben had educated her on the various species of trees including evergreen spruce, pine-oak, and the like. He had seemed genuinely pleased to share his knowledge of nature. And for that alone, the fatigue was well worth it.

"Puts things into perspective, doesn't it?" Reuben said softly, eyeing the display before them, almost speaking to himself.

Cathy nodded but could only wonder what perspective that

might be. Reuben was, of course, not the easiest person to read. She had first learned about his love of nature during their middle school trip the previous year, also to the Smokies. She knew that he had wanted to return, and to grant him his wish, Cathy had pestered her parents for months that they were due for a weekend getaway. The meteor shower forecasted this evening helped convince them, but they had no idea that Cathy would very indiscreetly invite Reuben—their neighbor and her classmate, alongside his uncle and aunty—which made for a rather awkward arrangement. As for the celestial spectacle itself, Cathy was hopeful that she would still be able to share the moment with only him, a plan already paved out by their very late departure from the cabin. She anticipated the meteors to ornament the evening sky in three hours' time, which meant she had to either delay their return from Newfound Gap or slow their ride back to Gatlinburg.

"Thanks for the invite," Reuben said. "You're a good person, Cathy."

"You're very welcome," Cathy responded shyly. "You know, if you want—"

A sudden breeze cut her sentence short, at the same time prompting Reuben to slip on the hood from his jacket. "What were you saying?" he asked.

"Oh, never mind."

He smiled at her, and then helped her to her hood, too. "The wind is chilling here," he said.

As Reuben turned back to the view of the mountains, which intrigued him so, Cathy felt a pinch of jealousy. His brown eyes were glittering in both peace and appreciation as he watched the natural world flow him by. It was shameful, as a young lady, to admit that she wished for his attention, at least a little more of it.

It was unthinkable that matters would turn out this way two years ago, that she would fall so hopelessly in love and yet not have any of it reciprocated or even noticed. She had been the class representative throughout middle school and now also in high school. Throughout her entire school life prior, she had been regarded as intelligent, sensible, rational, and also physically attractive. Sure, playing it cool was merely a front. In truth, high school was all sorts of excitement. People were aware of what they had in their wardrobes as well as the latest technology that one could wear. In the past year, the iPod had been the device to own and show off. But nothing interested people more than the gossip about who was dating whom.

Everyone was focused on the same things. It was really just a host of children trying to be precocious, Cathy included.

But he was different.

Reuben Granger was actually mature. Hailing from New York, Reuben was African American, his darker skin a conspicuous contrast to everyone else. Cathy hadn't thought much about racism. She didn't think her classmates were racist. But in Maryville, a predominantly "white" city, racism did in fact exist.

Reuben hadn't made it easy for himself, however. It was almost like he didn't want to belong with his outward arrogance and complete disinterest to participate in any activities. It had made Cathy's job as the class representative that much more

difficult. Cathy had not once been ostensibly mean to anyone, least of all Reuben. But at the start, she had hated him.

Nightfall had bestowed them roughly an hour into their return journey. Car headlights blinded their path from time to time, polluting the area with excessive light along with unnecessary honkings of the car horn that disturbed the silence of the mountains. As time passed, though, the number of driving visitors were evidently in decline—most people likely eager to return to the comfort of log cabins or whatever fancy accommodation they stayed at. Thankfully, the sky was still clear, allowing for the adornment of hundreds of stars and a vibrant waning crescent to naturally illuminate their path. Cathy had kept her eyes up for at least the past half hour, looking out for the slightest clue of when the meteor shower would come, almost passively pedaling behind Reuben, who appeared more interested in getting back to their families. The only obstacles blocking the expanse above were the towering trees and their thick canopies.

Reuben slowed down then. "Let's stop here for a small detour," he said.

Cathy paused in her track, not exactly sure what he meant.

"There's a clearance down here," he said, pointing to the woods. "A five-minute walk. We're late anyway, so we may as well settle for the view here."

"I didn't think you were interested," Cathy said, curling her lips into a smile.

"Why wouldn't I be?" Reuben said, already stepping off of his bike. "I'm sorry, though, about your parents. They're probably worried sick."

"No, they ... they know I'm a big girl. And besides, they know I'm with you, so—"

"And that's the problem," Reuben cut in. "Their prejudice would only grow after this."

"Wait," Cathy said with a slight frown. "You think they don't like you?"

"It's not about them, Cathy. Most people don't like me."

I like you, Cathy thought she said out loud. *And that's all that matters.*

Reuben was already on his way, stepping into the woods. "Let's go," he said.

Cathy parked her bicycle next to the road and then promptly trailed him. This was the moment. Everything was in place. She could ask for nothing better than the ambience, the isolation, and the incredible natural phenomenon that was about to befall them. She would confess her feelings. Or more hopefully, Reuben would confess his.

Even without the meteors yet, the current star-filled evening sky was breathtaking. Under such a display and situated deep within the tranquil woods, and more specifically away from any hints of human civilization, Cathy felt completely caressed by the evening landscape whose peacefulness was serenaded by the chirping of crickets and the soft hooting of owls. The woods could indeed pose various dangers, Cathy knew, as the school trip the previous year had suggested and stressed. From coyotes to black bears, and elks to skunks, the Smokies wouldn't fail to surprise. But with Reuben by her side, she feared nothing. He wouldn't only protect her, but he also would steer them well clear of any potential danger as if he had some kind of safety radar or simply an aura of goodness that repelled animosity from people and animals alike. Cathy knew it all sounded rather absurd, and yet she firmly believed that Reuben had special abilities that she was unable to define.

The promised five-minute walk was ticking away rapidly as a thousand words simulated in her mind. Before she knew it, they had arrived at a miniature valley with an opening above wide enough to sight the falling stars.

"Look!" Reuben urged suddenly, pointing to the north of the night sky.

Cathy lifted her eyes to where a thin stroke of white brushed down the black canvas, a vivid tail of stardust trailing its motion, the spectacle ending merely seconds following its appearance. The first meteor of the night. Short but spectacular, too short that Cathy didn't even remember to make a wish.

But soon came the second, the third, and the fourth—all of them scooting in and out of different directions, unlike the "shower" that Cathy had expected. Shining strokes of white—of hope and of dreams—flitted across every part of the canvas, flashing out almost as soon as they manifested. Cathy glanced across to Reuben whose expression was brightened up with a genuine smile, somehow a more attractive sight than the celestial spectacle itself.

"I'll remember this evening," Reuben said, as the last of the meteors faded away.

"Me, too," Cathy responded, ready to confess her feelings.

"I have a dream," Reuben said first, eyes still on the starry evening sky. "A dream to build dreams." He paused for a moment there, almost to allow Cathy some time to swallow the concept who instead tried repressing her urge for romantic intimacy. "Not everyone can reach for the stars," he then continued, "but I can help them. I will make every worthwhile dream come true."

Cathy swallowed, realizing that it was her turn to say something. "What... what do you mean?" she managed.

"Dreamscape," he said with a slight frown as he continued staring into the distance. "It's not possible for everyone to achieve their dreams in reality. And so, it is in their thoughts where I will plant and nurture their desires. It's in their minds where they will realize their aspirations. I wish to become an individual with true value, someone who might be remembered as having made a difference."

Cathy widened her eyes in admiration and slightly in embarrassment. "I think you can do it," she commented without too much thought. "I really believe it. You're so smart. You do well in everything."

"That's not true," Reuben said. "No one is good at everything. Dedication and focus are key if one hopes to truly excel in anything. I have limited skills in many disciplines including arts, music, and social science. But this is a conscious choice, as I have chosen psychotherapy—a field that helps me achieve my dream."

"Psycho... therapy?" Cathy repeated in confusion. "When did you... choose this?"

"About three years ago. I was still in New York at the time."

"And... you learn about this through self-study?" Cathy asked, flustered and almost incredulously, suddenly remembering the complicated drawings that she had seen him working on at the school library. "But what about regular school stuff? You know, like... ah..."

"The notion of romantic love fascinates people, as it does for me," Reuben said, seemingly having read her mind, now turning back to the stars. “However, to accomplish my objective, I am more than willing to give up anything and everything. Unfortunately, we simply cannot have it all, nor do I have such desire or ambition. I can do without friends and family, but I cannot live without my dream.”

Cathy’s eyes dilated even more as she watched him from behind, his figure, backdropped by the stars, suddenly so momentous and divine as if he were ascending to the heavens, perhaps to a place only he could reach. At that same moment, a violent torrent of memories from the past couple of years amassed suddenly into an understanding that she should have realized since the beginning, that Reuben Granger was indeed special—he was a genius. It had been silly to have ever considered him a peer, as *their* peer. The truth had manifested itself so ruthlessly now. Reuben was destined for greatness, for a destination that she couldn’t share the journey with, let alone help him reach. The gravitational pull he would eventually have on the human race as she had known it was inevitable. Cathy thought herself intelligent, but in comparison to regular people, not a prodigy. And this prodigy, Reuben Granger, had indeed been the same person since the first day she had met him. His intelligence was on a completely different level and his resolve had always been impregnable. How did Cathy possibly miss this, that anyone who dared to stand in his way was certain to be crushed and devoured by his roaring yet noble ambitions?

Later that evening as she laid in her cabin bed, Cathy brooded, crying softly into her pillow with the realization that it wasn’t nature that held Reuben’s attention—it was his dream. No one or thing could ever take precedence over his dream. And it wasn't even close.

FIVE

Broken Dreams

The more you know, the more you know you don't know. Less often said: the more you know, the more you want to know. Even less often said: the more you know, the more wrong you could be. Final word: sometimes, it is better to not know.

Twenty-five years was a long time. They called it a silver jubilee. Cathy had known Reuben for that long, since 2005. In this quarter of a century, however, they had been apart for more than they had been together. Maryville had never been the place that could offer Reuben what he wanted and needed. It had altogether been a surprise that he had elected to stay in Tennessee after achieving an almost perfect score on his SATs. His stint in UT Knoxville had been brief, however—only a year before he then made the move back to his hometown of New York City, after receiving a scholarship from Columbia University. That had been 2012. For seventeen years until the past year, there had been virtually zero correspondence between them.

For one thing, Cathy had frequently been on the road for at least the past ten years, with stops in California, Texas, and Colorado, working in various colleges as a professor in English literature. She couldn't pinpoint what it was exactly about commitment that gave her such acute apprehension, but every time when she had been offered longer contracts, she had instead submitted her resignation. The latest stop was New York, a place she had always gravitated toward, but resisted the urge for many years. The dream clinic—which was simply referred to on the advertisement as a general psychiatry practice, with the job title being general manager—had been the first job she applied for here. It was a high-paying job that was supposed to be something different for her, but also involving something she thought she would be good at—which was talking to people in a discreet and professional manner. Although she had thoroughly enjoyed her time working in the dream clinic—a little more than a year now—she had recently contemplated moving on.

Reuben actually treasured her as a close acquaintance, if not a friend. She still wasn't sure exactly what she meant to him. She remembered that back in 2012, he had done his part to keep in touch the old-fashioned way, with letters, and that he had written to her *three* times—all three of these letters stored securely in her childhood home in Maryville. But Cathy had never been able to scribble down any words in response, even with her natural aptitude for the English language, her skill level validated by critical acclaim of the articles she had written in the academic world. The feeling of having to write to Reuben, as she remembered it, had been far worse than writer's block. Now as she revisited the memory, Cathy suspected it was an ego thing. If she had kept in touch with him through the years, she would never have made it to this day. She would never have had any meaningful relationships with anyone other than her immediate family. Of course, the only one of those relationships that had survived till this day was her friendship with Beth, whom she had met a year after Reuben's departure from Tennessee.

"Ma'am!" a voice hollered. "You're blocking everyone."

Cathy turned her head, returning to her senses

immediately—also returning to the bright lights of the Walmart registers. She had been daydreaming in the line and was now holding everyone up. Promptly stepping forward, she apologized to the cashier lady and also to the customers behind her, some of them shaking their heads at the inexcusable injustice that was a result of her reverie.

Today was Wednesday, her only day off other than Sunday when the clinic was closed altogether. She didn't need any trouble. It was the day to reorganize her thoughts from all the emotions she experienced at work. And yet, running through her mind now were things that could potentially go wrong at the clinic in her absence. That was despite the fact that only the most straightforward clients were scheduled for Wednesdays, with the clinic open for business for only three hours and closing at noon. Toby could manage, Cathy told herself, especially with Reuben there if needed.

Reaching deep into her coat pocket for her keys, Cathy scanned the parking lot for her white Camaro, easily identifiable by its custom strips of silver on the convertible roof. Just as she reached the car, a rapid set of footsteps sounded from behind her, closing in on her. Cathy slid out her Swiss Army knife attached to her keys and then spun back to point the mini weapon at the intruder.

"Easy, easy!" said the man, middle-aged, dressed in a long trench coat.

It took several seconds for Cathy to place the stranger. And when she recognized him to be Sullivan, she felt no relief.

"What do you want?" Cathy asked with a squint, not yet lowering the pocketknife.

Sullivan glanced about at some of the people who had noted the commotion. "Can we act with some civility, please?" he asked. "I'm not here to hurt anyone. I just want to talk."

"I have nothing to say to you," Cathy said, holding back a snort, already turning back to her car. "If you insist, I'll have to—"

"I can tell you everything I know about Granger," Sullivan offered urgently.

Cathy paused for a moment, waiting for more.

"You're suspicious of his ways, are you not?" Sullivan asked. "I can help you fit the pieces together... on the condition that you help me."

He began fishing in his coat pocket for something upon sensing Cathy's continued distrust. "Here, look," he said, offering what looked like a small photo. "I'm no scam."

There were about seven or eight people in the photo, all of them in lab coats, inside a laboratory of some kind. Sullivan stood at the far right of the group with a friendly grin, and next to him was Reuben whose arm was wrapped around a girl—or perhaps only resting atop her shoulders.

Never had Cathy seen Reuben pose for any photos with a smile as genuine as this. Nor had she ever thought that he was capable of such intimate, physical contact in public. It was extraordinary still that the girl, behind a set of thick-framed glasses, was rather ordinary-looking. No, perhaps she *was* attractive, with her slim build, dark complexion and darker, wavy hair which dangled on one side over her lab coat. If one still considered race an important factor in relationships, the girl at least had this one advantage as an African American.

"Her name was Vanessa," Sullivan said with a sigh, seemingly having expected that the picture would silence Cathy. "His fiancée. Like Granger, Vanessa was a brilliant mind. This team here helped pioneer the beginnings of what you now call Dreamscape, but what it has become was never in our intentions. Even Vanessa, who made the breakthrough, wouldn't agree with his ways."

"Is she ...?" Cathy uttered anxiously, unable to complete the question.

Sullivan sighed with a nod. "Vanessa passed away in a traffic

accident three years ago."

Everything else that had led to the evening was a blur. As Cathy sat alone in the bay window of her apartment overlooking the bright lights of Manhattan, she thought carefully about Sullivan's words. The man had presented himself as the good guy, and Reuben as some kind of mad scientist. Normally, Cathy would instantly dismiss any negative idea about Reuben. For all she knew, Sullivan could have invented the entire story for the simple reason that he was bitter toward Reuben, perhaps because Reuben's achievements at Columbia University had far outshone him. Or, Cathy surmised as she squinted the city lights into a line of haze, perhaps it had something to do with Vanessa.

Sullivan had warned that any attempts at researching Vanessa was futile, that Reuben had erased all online evidence of her existence as it had been his only means to overcome his grief. The negative light in which Sullivan had described her childhood friend was shocking, and yet not completely implausible. Not only was Reuben selfish, according to him, but he was also incredibly obstinate in his ways, which in turn had resulted in the "conundrum" of the present day—the clinic, an establishment that represented everything "the team" had wanted to avoid.

Dreamscape helps solve nothing, Sullivan had said. *It is merely false hope. It will only exacerbate existing problems, visibly dissident from our core values of long-term, or even permanent solutions. There are no shortcuts in treating mental health issues. Reuben Granger knows this as well as anyone in the field, and yet, he elected to turn his back against his beliefs.*

Because of her. Vanessa. Her death has turned his world upside down. He is still running away. He couldn't accept the harshness of reality. And that, I believe, is why he is doing such stupid things. He no longer has any sympathy for anyone. Dreamscape is a business, a commercial product. Nothing more.

Not once had Cathy considered Dreamscape "stupid," but she hadn't defended the practice from Sullivan's barrage of criticism. It was a lot of information for her to process all at once. She was certainly still suspicious of Sullivan's story and any ulterior motive he might have. His intention, as he had claimed, was simply a request to Cathy, asking her to help guide Reuben back toward the "right path." In his own words, Sullivan actually described Reuben as a genius and someone he wished would again contribute to "their field."

Cathy had neither agreed nor disagreed to doing anything just yet. In any case, Sullivan had succeeded in making her think twice, making her realize that she had been deeply insecure about the blanked out seventeen years in which she had shared no correspondence with Reuben. How could she possibly know what he had experienced or what had become of him during this time?

For the past year, she had resisted the urge to undertake any kind of investigation, almost conscious of avoiding any topics which would bring up the past. It had been out of respect, to allow Reuben to share only if he was willing—like it had been when they were teenagers. Also, Cathy didn't think any self-respecting person would pry into another person's matters—unless if one was a tracker.

The vibration of her cell phone brought Cathy back into the moment of her empty apartment. Other than a floor lamp next to the couch, the only sources of light were the city lights from outside and her ringing cell, which displayed "Bethany" as the caller.

She slid the green "answer" icon to the right, and out popped the mini-Beth in a beautiful blue hologram. "Beth," she said first. "Can you arrange a meeting with Jackson? I want to track someone."

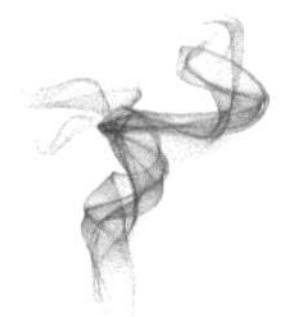

SIX
Playing with Fire

No one likes to listen to the skeptic, for they tell crazy stories. Skeptics challenge our ways of thinking, but we don't even bother. But what if they were right? What if our entire life purpose isn't what we believed it to be? After all, things might not always be as they seem. Even the brightest minds once believed the Earth to be flat. How can we ever be sure of anything when we can barely understand ourselves?

It was impossible not to sympathize with Martina, who at this moment appeared visibly excited on the rocking, nursery chair in the Dreamer's Lair, electrodes already attached to her temples. Every client had suffered some loss, of varying degrees. But as a woman, Cathy found nothing more heartbreaking than a stillbirth, and this was despite having never given birth. Martina's tragic loss had been almost four months prior, and while she had healed physically, her mental health had continued to deteriorate by the day. Her family, including the father of the dead child, had decided Dreamscape was their last resort for healing her deep wounds.

A simple flick of a switch put Martina into slumber. She was unconscious, as displayed by a small indicator on the ceiling screen. It was almost too simple, Cathy thought as she stared blankly at the screen which then exploded into colors. Unlike most others, Martina powered through the metaphoric nebulae and straight into her deepest desires, already seeing her baby child in her arms.

Cathy had slowed down the pace of the dream on display. She watched Martina cradling her baby in her arms with the most beautiful, natural smile between mother and child. But within echoed an unyielding voice. Sullivan's voice.

Dreamscape helps solve nothing.

It merely gives false hope.

It was true, perhaps. Martina was delighted now with her child in her arms, but the dream would eventually end, at which time she would be left with nothing again. Her child was dead. No matter what she dreamed, her child was still dead. That was possibly the reason why no one in the family even asked about being a part of the experience. In fact, they had seemed opposed to the idea of Dreamscape, one of them had mumbled about how technology had gone too far. They had left the building altogether after dropping Martina off, and still, they had seemed unsure that this was a good idea.

It exacerbates the problem.

Sullivan's voice again.

She's going to be devastated all over again.

Is that what you want, Cathy Reed?

A tingle of pain whizzed up along her spine as Cathy wondered just what would become of their latest client. *Your latest victim*, Sullivan added. She realized only now that this was the first time she had consciously questioned the morality behind Dreamscape and that of its inventor. In Reuben's defense, she reminded herself now, there had never been a single account in which a client had not awoken to more positivity and generally a more optimistic outlook to life. She remembered that Reuben had only ever explained this once—during the interview—that the purpose of Dreamscape was not to solve deep mental issues, but merely to allow patients to appreciate these issues from an unbiased perspective which in turn would allow them to recognize the inevitability, irreversibility, and sometimes, even the necessity of any unfortunate events. Apparently, this idea of simply relieving people of their neurotic unhappiness and nothing more was directly derived from Sigmund Freud's very own vision. And so at this moment, Cathy couldn't help but quietly curse at the so-called founding father of psychoanalysis.

It was difficult to maintain an air of calm when Cathy was growing more and more confused about exactly what Dreamscape was, more difficult yet *during* a dream session. And yet, she was still doing her best to make sure that she spared no unnatural glances at Reuben, although she *did* suspect for the first-time what Reuben's thoughts were—whether or not he really had no sympathy for anyone anymore. Would he care about what would become of Martina after today? Did he really see it as simply a piece of business, as Sullivan had suggested?

Of course, Cathy was also burdened with the guilt of having contracted Jackson to track Reuben. The only way to be sure that Reuben was still the same person as he had been in Maryville was to find the missing pieces from the blank years—the years they had been apart, which was more than they had been together. Sullivan was naïve to think he knew everything, Cathy believed, to judge Reuben based on incomplete evidence. He wouldn't know that more than twenty years ago, Reuben had shared with her—and possibly, *only* with her—his dream to build dreams.

No, Reuben was morally excellent. He was living his dream with the clinic, and his only intention was to help. Cathy was betting on Jackson to uncover all the evidence that would confirm this to be true.

On the screen that spanned almost the entire command center, Martina's child had already grown to school age, thanks to the fast-forward function. The girl's name was Ebony, and to Cathy, she was the most gorgeous child she had ever set eyes on. In the dream, Ebony had just returned from school, but had then set out again with Martina to a nearby park with their dog, a beagle. Ebony's innocent laughs, as she swayed back and forth on a swing, was a pleasing sound. Martina, who gently pushed her daughter from behind, was living in the moment, experiencing every cry of joy.

None of it is real, Cathy heard, the words whispered in that annoying voice again. *Everything is bound to implode.*

A soft pink tinge appeared before her then. Cathy looked up with a sniff, realizing that Reuben had handed her a tissue, also realizing that she had shed more than a few tears.

"I'm sorry," she said with another sniff, accepting the tissue and wiping away her tears.

"No need to be," Reuben said, stoic as always. "We're only human, after all."

Cathy giggled despite herself. "I'm glad you said *we*," she said. "Sometimes, you seem more than human."

Reuben paused and then offered a rare smile, seemingly finding humor in that comment. "In any case, it's getting late. Go now. Lock up for me."

It was already 8:30, and Reuben was strict that only unconscious people and himself were allowed on the premises after 9:00 pm. The only exception for a conscious person to remain was if they were under close supervision. Martina, meanwhile, was always going to stay the night as an unconscious patient, and her dream would play out harmoniously even on autopilot. But somehow, it didn't feel right to leave her here with Reuben, who ...

Who what? said Sullivan. *Go on. Elaborate your insecurities.*

Cathy held a fist and felt her brows knitting together in anger. *Shut up!* she demanded the inner voice. *All I am concerned about is Reuben's time. That it's too precious, that menial tasks such as this shouldn't be his job.*

Pleased about her resolve, Cathy rose to her feet. "Next time, allow me to do the night shift," she said to Reuben, who didn't spare her a glance.

"You know that's not possible," he said, "for legal reasons."

Of course, Cathy knew about the legalities about supervision of unconscious clients, that she couldn't do so unless she became qualified as a clinical psychologist. But she did truly wish to help Reuben out, if only to allow him to rest.

"All right then, I'm off. I'll see you tomorrow."

She stepped out of the command center and proceeded to close the clinic, switching off all the lights save a couple dim wall lights on either side of the lift which shone through the glass doors. Toby had left about a half hour earlier and had already sorted out everything needed for the next day. On the wall to the left of the wide reception desk was that poster she liked of the Carl Jung quote backdropped by an evening sky full of glow-in-the-dark stars.

Who looks outside, dreams; who looks inside, awakes, it read.

Cathy breathed in. *Be strong*, she urged herself, feeling rather peaceful in the dark. *And wake up. How can you possibly suspect him?*

Cathy stepped out of the clinic toward the lift, and just as she was closing the glass door behind her, her cell phone began vibrating insider her coat pocket. She held the door with one hand and fished for her cell with the other. She squinted at the "no caller ID" display but decided to answer it.

"What?" she said with an annoyance that surprised even herself, somehow certain she knew who it was.

"We really need to remedy those manners of yours, Ms. Reed."

Indeed, it was Jackson, the man she had been anticipating hearing from for several days.

She swallowed now, as she had dreaded this moment. "Do you have news?" she asked, more cautiously and softly.

"I'm a professional," Jackson said. "I always deliver. Anyway, enough of the pleasantries. Let's get to it." He paused for a second. "Your boss is an enigma. He's the most secretive person I've come across, and it appears that he has intentionally erased all the traces that might point to why and how he invented Dreamscape—which is only rational, to protect his intellectual property. But in saying so, he seems to be an expert at doing so—erasing those traces, that is. And that makes him rather suspicious of—"

"So, you're simply judging him based on your intuition?" Cathy cut in, naturally defending Reuben. "Did I pay you to hear your gut feeling?"

Jackson was silent for a moment. "I don't believe I'm the best person to judge one's ethics. I also can't say I know Reuben

Granger well enough to make any kind of accurate judgement of his character. Based on all the available information, I'd say he's ethical. But based on my *gut*—as you like to call it—I *don't* think he's ethical. It looks to me that he has more than his invention to hide. He wants to hide away a past that he himself is escaping from. And no, this isn't simply a wild guess. You would know that no one's allowed at the clinic after 9:00. But have you ever questioned why that is?"

"I've been here after 9:00," Cathy claimed. "Plenty of times. I stay the night. So have many clients. In fact, we have a client staying the night this very evening."

"Yes, but the clients are unconscious. Are they not?"

"They are, yes. But I'm wide awake when I stay. I know exactly what's going on."

"So you think."

Cathy snorted, growing more and more agitated. "You're telling me I don't know when I'm awake and—" She paused abruptly, suddenly recognizing what Jackson was claiming. "No," she said, "that can't be. You're saying that I'm somehow unconscious, too?"

"A wild guess, but yes. Based on your description of it, the clinic seems the perfect place to put someone to sleep. I don't know how the technology works, but with your blind fondness for Granger and all the sleep-inducing equipment available, I don't see that it would be all that difficult to put you to sleep."

"That's preposterous!" Cathy snapped. "I cannot believe I paid you all that money for such absurdity."

"He's hiding something," Jackson maintained. "I'm telling you. Look, I won't stop you from electing ignorance. But if you want to know the truth, you need to wake up—both literally and idiomatically."

Cathy hung up, grasping the cell tightly in quiet rage. A moment later after calming down slightly, she realized that her other hand was still holding the glass door. She stared at her gloved hand, which gripped onto the door handle, until her legs carried her back inside the clinic, as if moving independently from all her rational thoughts.

It was only 8:40, still twenty minutes to go. She quietly made her way behind the reception desk and then sank slowly into the chair—the dimness of the clinic helping her feel invisible. She watched the blank screen for a while, hesitant to switch it on, reluctant to do anything rash.

Her eyes began wandering about the walls and ceiling in search of anything that might indicate her presence. No one was to know she was still here. And certainly, no one was to know she would still be here after 9:00. After deciding that there were no cameras or other monitoring devices she didn't know of, she pulled out her cell again and opened the "SSD" app that Jackson had remotely installed without her permission on the day she reached out to him. With this app—which she had vowed not to use only days earlier—she could avoid having to set the alarm on the physical pad on the outside of the glass doors—and instead on the convenience of her cell.

SSD was neither commercially available nor well-known to ordinary people. The app itself, though, was owned and certified by Alphabet, the largest tech conglomerate in the world, and Cathy could only choose to trust that nothing of the clinic was being compromised. SSD itself stood for "Sign, Sealed, and

Delivered," primarily used for setting security devices. According to Jackson, and as she experienced now, the app was encrypted with many layers of security, but access was granted based on questions specific to each individual user. And specific, it was.

What was your first impression of Bethany Patterson? Answer in one word.

Envy, Cathy inputted, at the same time wondering how and when anyone could have recorded this information.

After several more personal questions, the app finally allowed her access to the clinic's alarm. Cathy was actually glad that some of the questions confirmed her as an employee at the clinic. In any case, she now turned the alarm on, as indicated by a dim flashing blue light at the glass door. She breathed a sigh of relief and then looked up from her cell to realize that she had, during her efforts to work out the app, snuck under the reception desk—a contemptible act of sneakiness she had never thought she was capable of.

She frowned, ashamed of herself. No matter how this ended, she wouldn't know how to answer to her own conscience anymore. If this was about—

Cathy froze then as footsteps sounded from the corridor, from the command center.

Her heart began to thump intensely, forcing her to push against the incessant pounding with a fist over her left breast. The volume seemed to almost tear apart the otherwise near silence of the clinic.

The footsteps, meanwhile, continued to approach. After all, there was only one way to go. And the dimness of the building served to amplify each thudding of the floor. Cathy shut her eyes tightly, not daring to catch a glimpse of Reuben, who might well discover her.

From the sound alone, Reuben stepped as close as a few feet away from the reception desk. He even stood there for a moment—in Cathy's sense of time, an eternity. And finally, when he began moving again, he receded down the corridor.

He didn't see her, it would seem.

Still, Cathy waited a few more minutes before she dared to move. She then slid carefully under the desk and looked first at the digital clock next to the computer monitor. It was 9:06. Without any hesitation this time, she proceeded to switch on the monitor that showed both the Dreamer's Lair and the command center.

As the white light of the monitor splashed at her, she covered her mouth with a hand. The command center was empty. In the Dreamer's Lair, meanwhile, was Martina, and across from her was Reuben in his lab coat, also with electrodes connected to his temples. Both of them were fast asleep.

SEVEN
A Turning Point

Everyone has a secret. Everyone should have a secret. And no one should share in it. But the word itself has a bad vibe and is usually associated with sinister causes. While it may well be, let us agree that it's not always so.

Cathy stared at the screen, unwilling to believe what she was seeing. Just what was Reuben doing? This had to be a dream, surely—her own. Since when was Dreamscape capable of running two different dreams at the same time?

Unless.

Cathy squinted specifically at the screen showing the command center, and more precisely at what the ceiling screens within displayed. Though the picture-in-picture all appeared rather vague, she made out that Martina's dream continued as normal—the heartbroken mother's visions displaying on one side of the connecting screen.

The other side of the connecting screen was ... blank.

It wasn't right. The screen should never be blank while in use. Was Reuben simply sharing Martina's dream, or was he somehow floating unconsciously within total darkness—was darkness itself his dream?

Cathy leaned closer in, almost smelling the monitor, her eyes further widening when the pitch black of Reuben's supposed dream gradually began taking some discernible form. Wisps of smoke puffed into view from all sides, rather randomly, followed by dark, grayish tendrils that slithered across the plane, gradually moving past Reuben rather than grasping him. Then, without any warning, the entire vision roared into color—albeit in dull colors, like old photographs.

Where was he now? Where was this dream taking him? Or, perhaps more accurately, where was he taking the dream?

A building.

My house!

Not her current apartment, but rather, her childhood home in Maryville. To Cathy's surprise, it was her—a teenage her—stepping out from the front door onto the porch, greeting Reuben with a half-smile. He had come to ask if he could borrow ... money? As the scene continued to progress, as if a film, Cathy was sure it was but a dream. Not once had Reuben visited her or even sought her out in any form, not now and not then. And money? She had never thought he had suffered from financial hardship. The real her was quivering, though, she noticed, as she wiped away a tear—of astonishment and of joy.

Cathy blinked away the blur, switched off the pixelated screen, and headed toward the command center. If she was going to do this, she might as well do it right. She hesitated for a fraction of a second at the high-tech door, in the fear that her access would be recorded. But her curiosity easily won over any rational concern. The entrance scan recognized her features next to instantly, and yet not nearly quick enough in relative time. When the door slid open, her eyes darted toward the wall-to-ceiling screens—not to the colorful east end of it which played Martina's dream, but to the west end filled with Reuben's dull colors.

It had been barely several seconds from the reception desk,

but the teenage her—or indeed, any form of her—was no longer being featured in the dream. In her place was *her*—Vanessa, Reuben's apparent research partner and fiancée. And indeed, they were in a lab, Reuben in the same lab coat he always sported at the clinic. They seemed to be working on an experiment of some kind, a hamster being their subject. Cathy turned up the volume from mute, and yet the details of their conversation were either too complicated or nonsensical for her to appreciate. It was a dream, after all. None of this might have happened. The theories being discussed possibly only made sense in a dream.

The one thing Cathy couldn't deny, however, was Reuben's outward joy in Vanessa's presence. Cathy hadn't noticed exactly when, but the overall dull colors from barely a moment ago had gradually turned more brilliant. Reuben had shown more emotions in a minute of the dream than he had shown in more than a year in reality, at least when in her presence.

Cathy blinked and then looked down to the controls, her eyes specifically in search for the time knob. It was strange, she thought then, that it had already been set to match the pace of real time.

Use the default settings until the dream has ignited, Reuben had said. *Otherwise, there might be complications.*

Reuben was never careless in the clinic. It was almost as if he had wanted this to happen, for Cathy to be here seeing all of this at this precise moment. But for what reason she did not know.

The dream fell silent rather abruptly. And when Cathy lifted her eyes toward the wall-to-ceiling screen again, she realized why.

They were kissing. Intimately. And the angle in which the scene was playing was at a super-zoom with high resolution.

Cathy blinked away in discomfort, searching aimlessly for another moment until her eyes fell on the time knob again. She proceeded to speed up time, now only seeing flashes of the dream in progression, nearly every part of it with Vanessa featuring prominently.

More images of Vanessa flashing on display further urged Cathy to turn the speed up. Watching this dream was a guilty pleasure, but also torture. And if Reuben had really arranged for her viewership, he was most certainly very cruel.

The flashing images ended abruptly, the dream on display reverting to real-time speed. Even the time knob clicked itself anti-clockwise into the slow position.

Vanessa was no longer in the dream, at least not in this scene. Reuben sat alone in the dark, at a bar-table inside what appeared an apartment kitchen. He was not himself, unshaved, his hair unkempt, his shirt untucked, one hand supporting his head while the other reached for a bottle of brandy. Visibly and acutely depressed, he then forcibly wiped away the alcohol which then smashed into pieces on the ground—the loud shatter causing Cathy to jump. With his other hand, which had actually been holding something, he threw a scrunched-up piece of paper at the kitchen wall.

Cathy swallowed as she sat back, assuming that something had happened to Vanessa—perhaps as Sullivan had claimed, that she had died.

It had been a traffic accident, Cathy recalled. On that thought, she turned the time knob into rewind mode as her eyes searched for any flashing images that resembled traffic accidents. She saw none, and then looked again for any hospital or funeral images. These existed, in bunches. She slowed the pace as she navigated to what appeared to be Vanessa's final moments, in which she wasn't conscious, laying in a wheeled bed with a score of bodies rushing her through corridors. Reuben was part of the mob, screaming at her to fight.

"Don't you dare bail out on me!" Reuben said, saliva flying out of his mouth, by far the most emotional and desperate Cathy had seen him.

No response from Vanessa, however, whose body was smeared with blood, her head locked in an immobilizer as she breathed through an oxygen mask. Even from the cockpit, Cathy was tearing up, noticing this when tears rolled down her cheeks. If the incident was as Sullivan had described, there was no hope for Vanessa. Of course, according to what had happened next in the dream with Reuben drinking himself into oblivion, the ending was effectively predetermined. Vanessa was going to die.

For the last time, Cathy looked away. She shut her eyes, squeezing out more tears. She inhaled deeply and then exhaled in distress, having taken in too many surprises in barely an hours' time. When she opened her eyes again, she headed toward the exit of the command center, and then stormed all the way out of the clinic, locking the entrance once more—this time manually from the outside before proceeding to the elevators—pressing the "down" button incessantly.

She held her head as she stepped into the elevator, now pressing the "first-floor" button more than necessary as well as the "close door" button. She wanted nothing but to go home and forget everything. But she also wanted to seek Sullivan. Or Jackson. Or Beth. Or return to Maryville. Or perhaps read up on dreams. Or the human psyche. Or how to deal with departed ones.

There were a thousand ors.

All of which seemed urgent and useless at the same time.

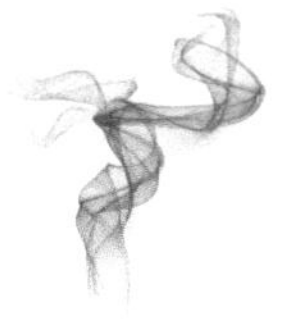

EIGHT

An Inconvenient Truth

Preconceptions are enormously powerful pointers. They are our inner compass. Where they might guide us, however, is anyone's guess. And any attempts to recalibrate this navigation device might only serve to further befuddle.

Sunday morning, 6:02 am.

In the face of the flashing colon of the digital clock, Cathy had managed only a few short bursts of troubled slumber. She remembered nothing of her dreams, or if she had any. Dawn was soon arriving, but behind the thick drapes that she had no desire to open, one couldn't know for sure.

Sunday. She focused on that. The day the clinic was closed.

A day of escape. A day in which she could perhaps think things through. She wouldn't see Reuben today. There would be no confrontation, at least until Monday.

Having refrained from checking her cell until now, Cathy frowned in noting that she had received no notifications, not even spam mail. Her fingers tapped at the browser icon and then typed in the search term, "escapism."

The concept itself was not unfamiliar to Cathy, having done research on the subject during her time at college. She disagreed that the idea of escapism was exclusively negative as was often portrayed in media, especially with the rise of virtual reality, usually regarded as the ultimate form of escape. Instead, Cathy had long believed that imaginary worlds—at least those in fictional literature—served to encourage creativity, which in turn was arguably the most sought-after skill in the modern job market.

And yet, it was difficult to apply any of this logic when it came to Reuben, who could hardly be considered ordinary. The man simply could not be categorized into the same standards as anyone else. Even if he were essentially doing the same thing as millions and millions of escapists, a new, more superior term should be coined solely for him. Cathy couldn't pinpoint what it was, but she was sure that Reuben had good reasons for everything he did, and what she had witnessed the previous night was no exception. She was deeply troubled, however, by the potential high frequency in which Reuben journeyed into Dreamscape and the dangers of not returning.

After clicking through links within links of superficial information, she came across an old psychoanalysis forum with posts by Sullivan. "Living in dreams" was the thread's subject line, started by... "Vanessa"—though this was merely a username. It could be *the* Vanessa, but it could also be someone else called Vanessa, as well as anyone else assuming her name. Sullivan's username, meanwhile, was "J. Sull," but somehow Cathy was sure this was him. Another five users were part of the public two-page conversation, all posts dated between July and September 2018—twelve years ago. Assuming that this was the same Vanessa she had seen in Reuben's dreams, Vanessa should be about her age, which in turn meant that at the time of posting, Vanessa was in her early twenties.

In any case, the thread discussed—or, more precisely, through some heated exchange, vehemently *argued*—whether deep, guided dreaming could solve one's inner troubles, or at the other extreme, misguide one into an abyss of no return. To Cathy's surprise, Sullivan and Vanessa were on the same side, preaching the former and that it was essential for psychoanalysts to develop technology to aid guided dreaming. The opponents, meanwhile, warned against the terrible dangers of meddling with what they believed should be left alone by all means, one of the posts concluding strongly that, *The deepest depths of the mind were never supposed to be discovered, let alone probed. We will find no answer there, only more questions and dark secrets that if unleashed unto the world, chaos shall reign.* Arrogant and unfounded, Cathy decided as she read, at the same time renewing her pride for having proven these naysayers wrong during her year of productive work at the clinic.

But Sullivan, if this was really him, why had he changed his stance?

Cathy sat up from her bed, scrolling down to the final post, dated September 17th, 2018, authored by Sullivan who had continued to fervently advocate for what would have been the infancy of Dreamscape. He had seemed a reasonable man then, but that was twelve years ago. There was no reason to believe that he was still reasonable, that anything he had said to her in the Walmart parking lot were true.

Cathy squinted at the text until she widened her eyes in shock as a new post, dated today at this precise time, suddenly popped out right below the one she had been reading.

Well done for getting here, it said, the poster being J. Sull. *I assume you finally recognize the danger he is placing others into as well as the dangers Dreamscape poses to himself. If you want to save him, we must act now. I would like to...*

As the words continued to appear one by one as if a sinister message from a horror movie, Cathy knew only to immediately switch off the network on her cell. She dropped the cell on the sofa and then stamped her way to the modem and ripped out the cable from the device, instantly departing all forms of herself from digital space.

She drew in a deep breath, and while exhaling, she collapsed onto the floor and against a wall, holding her head with both hands, shivering to a coldness that had been tormenting her from within. It had only been nine or ten hours prior when all had been right with the world.

She closed her eyes tightly, her hands now clenched into fists with nails digging into her flesh, searching for some form of sanctuary, knowing well it was all in futility.

Reuben, she thought with gritted teeth as she battled with the disarray and the physical pain, *who exactly are you? What have you become?*

And... what have I become?

Vanessa, you bitch! What did you do?!

How dare you break him? How dare you die on him?

This is all your fault! If you weren't already dead, I'd be sure to—

A massive double door slammed down from the sky before her with a deafening clap, ending the soliloquy abruptly. Other than the giant metal door which was the height of at least three grown men, all around her was an infinite space of white in which she and the door were floating in. All was silent.

This had to be a dream. And in fact, it was rather welcome that she had finally fallen into slumber. The only wish now was

the force coinciding with a distinct creaking sound, blinding light seeping in.

"No, don't!" Cathy pleaded, reaching her arm out.

The girl paused and slowly turned her head, revealing her true identity behind the flash of light from the other side of the door, her face being a fearful confirmation of what Cathy had suspected. The girl was her—a younger her at about ten years of age, innocent and carefree.

"I know you're scared," young Cathy said in what most would consider a sweet voice. "I am, too. But he needs our help."

"I don't know enough to help!" Cathy confessed. "I don't even know what to help with, or what needs helping! *I* need helping, too!"

"This has never been about you," young Cathy responded, with little care for older Cathy's wellbeing. "We exist for his sake. You are worthless individually, so please don't be selfish."

Cathy shook her head, unable to comprehend what her younger self was saying. And before she conjured any ridiculing response, a second figure appeared next to young Cathy.

"I also existed for him," said the newcomer whose dark complexion glowed beneath her light-colored dress.

"Vanessa?"

"My death was a tragedy, but I am deeply honored to have been a part of Reuben's life, and to have assisted in guiding him toward this path."

"And what path is that?" asked a third person—Sullivan, appearing to the immediate left of Cathy herself, but stepping toward Vanessa. "Self-destruction? Even in death, you still willfully elect ignorance when it comes to Granger."

"And you still fail to understand the significance of who Reuben Granger is," Vanessa responded. "Unlike you and me, his legacy will live on forever."

"He is perceptive, I'll give you that," Sullivan said. "But if things continue as they are, who will carry on the legacy?"

"We will," said young Cathy. "Me and her," she said, nodding at older Cathy in clarification. "That's a promise."

"Thank you," Vanessa said with a smile, holding onto young Cathy's hands.

Vanessa then turned to older Cathy. "Goodbye," she said, and together with young Cathy, they turned toward the double door and thrust it open with a non-contactable swipe, allowing the blinding radiance from within to shoot out voraciously into all directions of the meadow. Cathy could only cover her eyes from the intensive glare.

Only when the door closed shut with another thundering thud, taking the brilliance with it, did Cathy look up again. The pleasant hue of the daytime meadow had been restored. Cathy was all alone again—somehow, even Sullivan had disappeared. Even if it were merely a dream, it was a strange one. But was it only a dream?

Wake up, Cathy told herself. *Wake up now.*

With impressive calm and composure, Cathy opened her eyes slowly and carefully to the reality of her apartment again. She was still in the same spot as she had been when she fell asleep. The clock displayed 9:43 am, in other words a three-hour sleep. She curled up, wrapping her knees with her arms, her head resting between her kneecaps.

Intuition told her that the dream she had just woken up from had been more than that, that it had been a premonition of some kind. But what? If one could indeed find answers in dreams, then perhaps this deserved some careful analysis. What did the door represent? Why did her younger self represent? And what did all the dialogue mean?

Cathy started then as a buzz sounded. It was her doorbell. But rather than relief, it was surprise and a hint of dread that washed over her. Her visitor was Reuben.

NINE
Perpetual Struggles

How does one even begin to attempt formulating an answer to the meaning of life? Even the most successful and fortunate, the happiest and wealthiest, eventually wither away to dust as if they never existed. Is it not absurd to be born into this eternal cycle of what some consider as atonement of our sins? I invite you on this journey to find out. It will be worth your while.

This was the same restaurant in which the interview had taken place more than a year prior. Jean-Georges, an upscale French eatery in Manhattan. This marked only the first time since then that they were sharing a meal. And the first time since seventeen years ago that Cathy had seen Reuben not in a lab coat, instead sporting a regular overcoat.

"Again, sorry to have kept you waiting," Cathy said, her third apology this morning. "I know how impatient you are."

"That I am," Reuben admitted with a cough as he reached for his glass of sparkling water, the transparent liquid striking with brilliance under the natural light that filled the eatery through the floor-to-ceiling window overlooking Central Park. "But Cathy, let me be the one to apologize. I have let you down. I have not been myself... for a long time. And for that, I owe you an explanation."

Cathy met his eyes, but said nothing, waiting for more. She had indeed taken her time this morning—more than half an hour—in making herself presentable. She was certain that Reuben didn't see her in *that* way. And given the high likelihood that her childhood friend had neglected the ethical codes of professional psychiatry and was hence no longer able to uphold the integrity of what she believed Dreamscape represented, there should have been far more pressing matters to consider than how she looked. No matter, Cathy owed it to the teenage girl inside of her.

"My old acquaintance," Reuben said. "Jeremy Sullivan. It has been a few weeks, but I believe he is still on your mind. Do you want to know more?"

Cathy swallowed. "Well, yes, actually. But why all of a sudden? Why now and not when he appeared?"

Indeed, she wondered, as her hands sweated heavily under the table, whether Reuben knew that she spied on him the previous night.

Reuben inhaled deeply, but his lips then curled into a smile. "You should know that I am neither the most sociable person nor the most trusting. I am also not great at reciprocating any kind of favors. It was during my slumber last night ..." he said, pausing briefly, sending a shiver down Cathy's spine as he looked deeply into her eyes, "that I learned, or relearned something—your professional, dedicated service for the clinic—which, incredibly, pales in comparison to the constant friendship that you offer—that you *have* offered to me since I was a child ... back in Maryville."

He paused again, inhaled deeply once more. "I would very much like to earn your genuine support. I want your help. And to do so, I need to be honest with you."

"I appreciate that," Cathy uttered finally, doing her best to appear collected. "All right then, can you please start with Sullivan?"

"He was a research fellow with whom I worked with at Columbia University," Reuben explained, looking out to the panoramic view of Central Park as if in reminiscence. "The idea of Dreamscape was my own, but he was a vocal supporter as well as an invaluable member of the research efforts—at least at its infancy. His aggressive behavior that evening stemmed from our falling out years ago, which in turn was a result of our differences in opinion. He hoped to employ Dreamscape in a way that was dissimilar to my own, and hence our disagreement and eventual severance."

"All ... right," Cathy said, struggling to hide her suspicions. "Then in what way was he thinking we could use Dreamscape?"

Reuben downed another mouthful of the sparkling water, coughing again. "Allow me to first say that he is a brilliant man in his own right," he continued, meeting Cathy's eyes again after wiping his mouth with his napkin. "His vision for Dreamscape, however, was limited in that it should only be used for the treatment of patients with traumatic mental issues."

"And is that not precisely how we have been using it?"

Reuben squinted in mild disapproval. "Superficially, yes," he said. "I am surprised you would think that after witnessing firsthand how it is being used."

"I agree that it has been employed for wider use—giving hope to people who have lost it—helping people achieve dreams that they might otherwise be unable to in reality. Yes, I recall that you once said that Freud believed that psychoanalysis is only to relieve people of their neurotic—some call *crazy*—emotions. But surely, our best work ... it's to help those who are traumatized, to show them that life is valuable, that it's always the preference over death.

Is it not?"

Reuben said nothing for a moment, then shook his head. "It is not," he said finally. "To lift others from pain is noble. It is morally excellent. But that is secondary to what I have always envisioned."

"And what *exactly* is it that you envision?"

Cathy only realized that she had notched up the volume when the waiter, neat as the most immaculate butler, paused next to their table with a slight frown. Some of the other customers shot some disapproving scowls of their own in their direction, too, to which Reuben seemed unbothered by.

"My vision is ..." he said, composed as always, "the transcendence of the mundane, relentless struggle of everyday life, from this existence—to evolve into a higher form of being."

Cathy stared now, dumbfounded by the surprising, preachy-spiritual talk.

"Thoughts are immensely powerful," Reuben continued. "But thoughts cannot nurture themselves. It is through knowledge—science and philosophy, in particular—in which our mind and consciousness can blossom. This is the very reason we study, and why the Age of Enlightenment of the eighteenth century is marked as a critical movement in the history of mankind. There is no meaning in helping one or two individuals 'get back on their feet'—excuse the colloquialism—when the struggle for so-called happiness is perpetual and without hope of success. This is the fundamental problem with the human condition. Intellectuals may one day solve all the world's existing problems, but as they undertake this very noble attempt, an abundance of new problems will arise. There is no ending. There is no meaning."

Cathy frowned slightly, growing more confused. "And the solution is ... ?"

"I cannot say we now possess the knowledge to efficiently complement our thoughts," Reuben said. "But modern humans, having walked the Earth for three hundred thousand years, should certainly contemplate the next step. To me, it is through our consciousness where we can find answers, or at least clues on how we might proceed. With Dreamscape, we have the technology to observe the deepest depths of the human psyche—which I repeat, is immensely resourceful. I envision a nebulous dream in which we can drift about for eternity."

"I ..." Cathy said, struggling to find words, "I did not expect this."

Reuben grew more relaxed, leaning in slightly. "And what *did* you expect?"

"I don't know!" Cathy said quietly but in agitation, turning toward the outdoor view. "I'm just an ordinary woman. I think about things like what to eat on a Saturday night, which ... shoes of the newest season I should buy, and ... uh, where to go for my next holiday. Not something so absurd like how we can *evolve* as beings!"

"Absurdity lies in the predicament of everyday life," Reuben said, still with his signature air of calm. "The struggle of living, to find meaning ... to create, cause, solve, ignore, and accept problems which arise in the mundanity of life is the very definition of absurdity."

Cathy had no response to that. After a brief intermission, she asked instead, "Can you tell me about her? About Vanessa?"

Reuben's expression changed immediately, his brimming confidence suddenly replaced by a slight frown of melancholy. "She was my wife," he said, the claim incredible to Cathy. "Not legally recognized, but personally so. She was my soulmate ... my research partner, colleague, classmate, best friend, and partner in life."

"What happened to her?" Cathy asked, unable to restrain herself.

Reuben straightened up, seemingly having already recovered from what had been a very brief collapse of emotional control. "She passed away in a car accident," he said calmly.

"Are you ... over it?"

Reuben scoffed quietly this time. "No," he said. "There is not a single day in which I do not think about her. And yes, dwelling on it achieves nothing, and so I have sought *professional* help from a few renowned psychiatrists. Nothing worked, unfortunately, and I no longer see anyone."

"You went to psychiatrists ... ?" Cathy asked, almost unwilling to believe it. "Why didn't it work?"

"I know more than them," Reuben said. "More about psychiatry."

"But I think, maybe ... just maybe—"

"She was carrying our unborn child, four months into her pregnancy," Reuben added, cutting Cathy short, almost like a stroke of lighting tearing apart the night sky. "No amount of professional help can help me get over that."

Everything fell silent and still once more.

Cathy turned away toward the window, her eyes flooded with tears, wandering across the panorama of Central Park as she attempted to digest the information. This she did not know. And it hurt. Sullivan never mentioned that. Perhaps even he didn't know. Inside, she was sorry that she had ever thought a negative thought about Vanessa. Tragedy naturally brought sympathy, and sympathy was something that Cathy was never great at coping with.

She could hardly find the courage to turn back to Reuben just yet, and as she tried, she also wondered what else there was to say and how this session would end. She started then when suddenly Reuben rested a hand on her own, which she had left tapping the table. She looked at him again, sincerity filling his face. He then slid a classic paperback across the table toward her.

"A gift," he said. "From me to you, and eventually from you to me."

Cathy said nothing, though squinting down to the title to see that it was *The Myth of Sisyphus*.

Albert Camus? She was almost certain that she had read Camus in the past, maybe even this title. And in truth, she would gladly read any literature book, especially when recommended by Reuben. But she wasn't so sure if the condition was that he wanted her to decipher some hidden message from within.

TEN
Eternal Sleep

To achieve any success in exploration, one must let go. One must prepare for no return. More times than not, the destination is unfruitful even if one gets there. But an attempt is a chance, as opposed to no chance. Go. Document your findings. Pass it on. The next in line or the one after might well complete the journey you began.

This was only the third time that Cathy had spied. The first time was a revelation. The second was a confirmation. Perhaps Reuben knew and perhaps he expected this. She didn't think he knew, however, that today—the third and final time—was *the* day to say goodbye. She doubted that he would know the exact date when she would make her move. Intelligent and wise, he was. But Reuben was no mind reader—only a guide in this instance, a guide who had led Cathy through twenty-five years of life without her knowing, all the messages she had received from him since 2005 had ultimately been a solemn and sincere request to have this done today. Cathy looked into the screen, knowing well that this was the end, watching Reuben and their client both sitting in slumber, dreaming separate dreams with electrodes attached to their temples. Only one of them was going to wake up.

In any case, the month-long plan had finally come to fruition, all of which began on the day at the French eatery. Through Cathy's careful deliberation, the clinic was to close for two weeks, this information known to no one except for Toby, who would not have to report for work during this time. Toby had left at about 6:00 pm. For all Toby knew, there was a two-week break, a transition period in which Reuben would transfer the practice to Cathy. The young receptionist believed it when Cathy told him that Reuben, who had always preferred solitude, had chosen to retire. He didn't even ask questions or say goodbye for the last time simply because the two men rarely shared a word anyway. Cathy was sure that Toby admired Reuben for his intelligence, but ultimately didn't like him as a person.

Cathy recognized only in this past month that this had all been part of Reuben's plan, that by giving her full responsibilities for accepting and prioritizing clients on the waiting list, he was effectively passing on the baton. It was no surprise, therefore, that Reuben hadn't even looked ahead to their schedule since the day he had relinquished control of picking clients.

Current circumstances would allow Reuben to sleep—and dream—for an estimated five days while living on only water and nutrients, fed to him with the hospital-grade equipment Cathy had borrowed from Beth. Cathy also owed her neuroscientist best friend for spending days explaining to her how the brain worked scientifically, which in turn allowed her to see that her actions tonight were inevitable. Beth knew nothing of what she was about to do, of course, and she had been trusting enough not to ask further questions—not even about why she needed the coma equipment—only warning her not to do anything stupid. Even now, a part of Cathy considered all of this to be very stupid.

It was also illegal in every respect of modern law. But none of that mattered in the bigger picture. Reuben was assured of up to five days of sleep, equating to almost a hundred lifetimes in dream state—all before he would leave this world forever. This was the "nebulous dream" he had quoted, a place he could drift about eternally. Hopefully, it was enough for him to reach the greatest depths of his consciousness and find the answers he sought. Cathy's job was critical, too, in that she was the witness to potentially incredible discoveries. She would hold the key to and perhaps lead a paradigm shift in the way people think about consciousness.

Cathy looked up at the display now, which had already been adjusted to match real time. She was glad to know, even as a cameo, she featured in almost every one of Reuben's dreams. There was nothing particularly sensible about the dream at this very moment, just random people including her floating about, into and out of Reuben's vision. Cathy exhaled and watched for a moment longer. She then stood from her seat and stepped out of the command center and all the way to the Dreamer's Lair. She paused at the door, almost forgetting that a client was still with them, watching only Reuben under the dim lighting. He was still here with her. She didn't have to go ahead with the plan.

Battling with her conscience, she proceeded toward Reuben, sitting on the seat next to him and attaching electrodes to her own temples. She had already set the timer on this ahead of time. She was going to share his dream for the duration of twenty minutes of real time.

She closed her eyes and opened them again to find herself ... in school. This was Maryville. Cathy was her current self rather than the junior high student version who shared the room. The class had been dismissed, it seemed. Only a handful of students remained, for no apparent reason—though reason itself was usually incompatible with dreams. Reuben, the boy version of him, was one of the students in the classroom. He was reading a book—uncommon for anyone to dream about. And the text was far more sensible than any other text she had seen in all the dreams she had been involved in. It was a novel, an old one. *Candide* by Voltaire.

Knowing well that it was generally unwise, dangerous even, to interact with anything inside someone else's dream, Cathy stepped toward the young Reuben.

Are you enjoying the philosophy? she asked, to which Reuben lifted his innocent brown eyes from the novel.

I am, he said. *The satire, too.* He tilted his head slightly. *Ma'am, you remind me of someone.*

Cathy turned back, but her younger self in the dream had left—disappeared.

It's getting late, young Reuben said. *Here, please take this as a gift. It is always a pleasure to meet someone who shares your values. Let us meet again.*

And that was it. He left, the entire classroom vanishing immediately into nothing following his departure. All that was left was an infinite dark space of emptiness, but also the book. Cathy opened it, flipping through a few pages until she found a written note inside.

The essence of the practice is the technology, to which I shall leave with you, it read. *Thank you.*

Cathy opened her eyes again, returning to reality. She rose to her feet and watched Reuben, still immaculate even in slumber, still sporting his signature lab coat all so proudly. She brushed her fingers across his face, feeling his physical existence one last time.

"Goodbye," she said, and then kissed his forehead.

Very gently, she moved behind him and disconnected him. Without another glance, she stepped out of the room, returning to the reception desk rather than the command center. Feeling heat in her eyes blurred slightly by tears, she caught sight of the book that Reuben had given to her. *The Myth of Sisyphus*. She had read it twice since receiving it. If there was a hidden message inside the story related specifically to Reuben, it was probably that Reuben *was* the Greek king. Like Sisyphus, Reuben had worked tirelessly and in eternity. And even in death, he was to continue.

ACKNOWLEDGEMENTS

Dreams has always been a topic of fascination to me. But in more recent years, I have wondered particularly about how dreams might affect what and how people think—not exactly one of the latest mysteries-of-life-questions if you have watched a certain Leonardo DiCaprio film, which is not where any elements of this novella is from. The concept of thinking or reasoning is the cause of many factors. There's intelligence, wisdom, experience, personality, and religious and political alignments. And then there's dreams, or perhaps intuition. All these circumstances affect us, and in turn, our individual opinions differ. Ultimately, we find most others odd and intolerable. I do sincerely hope that we practice a little patience.

The novella's central theme of professionally making dreams in a controlled environment was indeed from a dream of my own, but from quite a while ago. I cannot remember exactly what happened in that dream except that there was some kind of lab, or maybe a factory, where different dreams were stored in boxes moved along on a conveyor belt to ... nowhere—probably in an infinity loop. I must have noted down some more detailed content at the time, and what I remember of it now is probably more from what I *think* I dreamed rather than what I actually dreamed. Nonetheless, it is my unconscious mind which I extend the most credit for this novella.

In terms of the writing, David Kent is the man I owe my gratitude to. A true professional in editing. The art was done by Caring Wong, whose skillful blending of colors, allowed me to see parts of the original dream come true.

FINAL WORD

Thank you for reading *Into a Dream*. If you enjoyed it, I'd be grateful if you could leave a short review on any platform that suits.

Novellas and contemporaries are not usually my thing. This was more of a side project from the epic fantasy series I am writing. I certainly did enjoy writing this, however, and do hope to write similar works in the future. Some writers find it criminal to cross between genres, but I find the process very natural, really. Genres, to me, is a guide rather than a rule. I feel that if I have a story to tell, I can tell it in any genre.

Finally, if you made it all the way to this last page, I kindly ask you to consider picking up my epic fantasy series *Memories from Oblivion*. You can also find out more on:

www.atlas-hill.com

Thanks again for reading.

C:\Users\DELL\AppData\Roaming\Microsoft\Templates\
al.dotm
itle: Into a Dream
ubject:
uthor: Atlas Hill
eywords:
omments:
reation Date: 21/11/2019 8:57:00 PM
hange Number: 5
ast Saved On: 21/11/2019 9:09:00 PM
ast Saved By: Alan Ho
otal Editing Time: 12 Minutes
ast Printed On: 21/11/2019 9:10:00 PM
s of Last Complete Printing
Number of Pages: 90
Number of Words: 19,248 (approx.)
Number of Characters: 109,720 (approx.)

www.ingramcontent.com/pod-product-compliance
Lightning Source LLC
Chambersburg PA
CBHW060759310726
48980CB00002B/161

9780648285243